dead or alive?

☆   ☆   ☆

Lex could hear voices but they were far away and indistinct. He was floating, and tried desperately to open his eyes. The voices faded in and out, sometimes sounding as if they were coming from some place right behind him, then going away again, faint echoes that he knew he should be able to understand, if only the people would come closer.

His ears rang, and his head felt as if it was spinning. He couldn't feel his body anymore, not even the pain in his left shoulder. Everything was wrapped in something thick and soft, like the old comforter full of goose down his grandmother had given him so long ago. He tried to visualize her. Something, he thought it must be a face, started to materialize in the distance, and he tried to move toward it. It floated, silent as a hawk high in the sky, but the harder he tried, the more helpless he felt...

★

Also by
Dan Mason

THE RANGER
BORDER BANDITS
COMANCHE RAIDERS

**Published by
HarperPaperbacks**

DAN MASON
THE RANGER
RANGE WAR

HarperPaperbacks
A Division of HarperCollinsPublishers

If you purchased this book without a cover, you should be aware that this book is stolen property. It was reported as "unsold and destroyed" to the publisher and neither the author nor the publisher has received any payment for this "stripped book."

This is a work of fiction. The characters, incidents, and dialogues are products of the author's imagination and are not to be construed as real. Any resemblance to actual events or persons, living or dead, is entirely coincidental.

HarperPaperbacks *A Division of* HarperCollins*Publishers*
10 East 53rd Street, New York, N.Y. 10022

Copyright © 1991 by HarperCollins*Publishers*
All rights reserved. No part of this book may be used or reproduced in any manner whatsoever without written permission of the publisher, except in the case of brief quotations embodied in critical articles and reviews. For information address HarperCollins*Publishers*, 10 East 53rd Street, New York, N.Y. 10022.

Cover illustration by Larry Schwinger

First printing: November 1991

Printed in the United States of America

HarperPaperbacks and colophon are trademarks of HarperCollins*Publishers*

10 9 8 7 6 5 4 3 2 1

1

LEX Cranshaw was dead tired. It had been a grueling ride from Deguello, and the July sun hammered the plains hard enough to flatten the endless waves of grass. The trail, little more than a trickle of dust kicked in the ground, bordered on either side by blades seared a sickly yellow by the long drought, speared straight ahead for as far as the eye could see. Somewhere up ahead lay Laidlaw, Texas. If it had a hotel, he would stay over, give himself the luxury of clean sheets and a long soak in water a little too hot. If not, he'd settle for what he could find. His shoulder hurt like hell. As far as he could tell, he had stopped bleeding, but he felt weak, sometimes thinking he was going to slide right out of the saddle.

He was on the edge of civilization, but civilization in these parts was Texas style, and that meant rough edges.

He was used to it, but there were times when he felt older than the endless hills surrounding him on every side. The bullet wound in his arm didn't help. It throbbed steadily, and the arm hung at his side like a dead fish on a string. He was used to that, too. It came with the territory. There even were times when he thought it came with being a man, as if pain and the ability to inflict it on others were the hallmarks of humanity.

As he rode, he kept his eyes fixed dead ahead, searching the sun-blurred edge of the planet for the first hint of shadow that would signal the presence of a town, any town. He had wanted to lie down, it seemed, for days, and about three hours earlier he had reached the point where he wouldn't have minded not getting up again. At least until he had to.

His skin felt dry and hot. That was only partly the result of the merciless sun. The rest was probably fever. The arm might be getting infected, and he knew the bullet was still lodged there, somewhere close to the bone. Behind him, more miles than he could now count, two mounds of earth, already dried to the same dull beige as the rest of the universe, marked the final resting places of two men, one a friend and one the man who'd killed him. When he thought of Jason Hartwell, his arm hurt a little less, and when he thought of the look in Cord Schuster's eyes—that glitter, bright as a new coin tossed high into the noonday sun—the pain went away altogether. But what took its place was another kind of throbbing, the incessant thump of rage pounding in his blood.

It was the first time Lex could remember taking pleasure in pulling the trigger. He didn't like feeling that way, hated himself for it, the way only a man who lived every day with his life poised on the curve of a trigger could. Jason Hartwell had been the nearest thing he'd had to a brother. But Jace was a Ranger and knew the risks. The life expectancy of a Texas Ranger was short, and it burned like a fuse. The closer you got to the Nueces Strip, the shorter it got.

And in Deguello, Cord Schuster had lit a match. Jace flared and went out. It was cold comfort that he'd gone out the way he would have wanted to, and none at all that the man who'd killed him lay a few feet away.

Lex shook his head, then glanced at the sun. For a moment, he stared at it; then he closed his eyes, letting the sun punch through their lids, turning the world into a red smear. It was well past noon, and Lex turned away from the heat. Opening his eyes again, he could see his shadow to his right, a blurry centaur riding through Hades, a brilliant gilding at its edges where the sun chewed away at the darkness, resenting even this small opposition.

Lex ran his right hand across his chin, feeling two days of stubble brittle as the nub ends of cornstalks. The skin of his palm whispered like rustling leaves. Without slowing, he reached for the canteen dangling from the pommel of his saddle and tugged the canvas strap free. Jamming the canvas-covered canteen up under his wounded arm, he winced, then chewed at his lower lip as he unscrewed the cap, every movement of the arm a small, hot knife scraping its way out from the bone. When the cap came free, he let it hang from the small chain, took the canteen in his good hand, and brought it to his lips.

He could taste the bitter salts, the white crust on the dull gray metal, even before the water dribbled into his parched throat. His tongue felt like a razor strop, his lips as if they would crack and peel away like dried mud from an old boot. The water was warm, almost hot, but at least it was wet. He swirled a mouthful, thought about spitting it out to rinse away the trail dust, but there wasn't that much left, and he swallowed, feeling the sand settle back between his gum and cheek as the water went down.

Cramming the canteen back under his arm, it hurt more this time, as if he had awakened some sleeping demon that lay there waiting for him. He gritted his teeth, feeling the scrape of sand against them, dropped the strap back over the pommel and closed his eyes, blinking away the tears.

The trail looked brighter somehow when he opened his eyes again. The water along the edge of their lids sparkled, outlining everything with small jewels. He blinked the tears away in time to see a black dot materialize out of nowhere far ahead. Behind it, a faint plume of dust, its color almost bleached away by the sun, slowly drifted away. The horseman was cutting at an angle toward the sun, and Lex felt his pulse quicken, sending one more painful sword slashing through his left arm.

There were four dots now, three in a clump well behind the first, but they were closing fast. Far away, he heard tiny snaps, which he immediately recognized as gunshots. He looked for the telltale puffs of gun smoke, but the dots were too small, the puffs smaller still.

He spurred his big bay stallion, leaving the trail and cutting onto the grass. He veered sharply, trying to cut an angle that would intersect the path of the horsemen. All four were still too far away for him to make out any details. He wondered if it was a small raiding party of Comanche or Kiowa, knowing they seldom came this far south anymore, usually slipping off the reservation for a few days, but never far enough that they couldn't get back in a day's ride.

As the dots slowly drew closer, they started to assume shape. He was close enough that the sporadic gunshots had that sharp, familiar crack now, and he could tell the pursuers were white men. No Indian ever wore a Stetson with that easy grace. The quarry was a white man, too, and he kept looking back over his shoulder. As far as Lex could tell, he hadn't fired a shot, and the Ranger wondered if the man was unarmed.

Lex drew his Colt and fired one shot into the air. He saw the blur of a white face as the lead horseman glanced his way and then, as if suspecting that Lex was in league with his pursuers, changed direction and headed due west into the sun.

Lex saw the gap shrinking and the small clouds of dust where stray bullets plowed into the ground. He fired again, but he might as well have been shouting into an empty sky. The loud crack of the Colt went unheeded. A second later the lead horse stumbled, staggered a few strides, then went all the way down. The charging gunmen reined in as their quarry rolled to one side. The fallen horse struggled to get up, but it had broken a leg, and its weight was too much for the wounded mare.

Lex expected the men to dismount. He shouted, but his words were drowned out by a volley of pistol fire. The unhorsed man fell in a heap. One of the horsemen fired once more, then jerked the reins and dug his spurs in. The other two followed suit. Lex shouted once more, this time provoking a gunshot aimed his way. The bullet sailed wide, but not so wide he didn't hear it whistle past.

A moment later the three horses were in full gallop, kicking up gouts of dry grass and drier soil as they made a wide arc and swung back the way they had come. Lex was still a hundred yards away from the mare, which continued to try to get up. The man lay motionless a few yards away.

Lex closed, dismounted, and let the reins drag on the ground. He winced with every step, reached the still form, already soaked in blood, and knelt beside it. The man lay on his side. Four bright red flowers continued to unfold ragged petals on the front of his faded coveralls. His eyes were open, but already beginning to glaze. Lex felt for a pulse, found nothing, and looked after the horsemen slowly dwindling back into the featureless black dots they had been when he'd first spotted them.

Shaking his head, Lex sank back on his haunches, then collapsed onto his butt, sitting there with a cold chill creeping down his spine. He'd seen murder before, even cold-blooded murder. But he'd never seen anything to match the brutality of what he'd just witnessed.

He found himself wondering who the dead man might have been. From the look of his clothes, he had been a farmer. The round face, its muscles slack in death, was open, even pleasant. A big man, rawboned, his skin that red-tinged copper so many recent settlers got from their first exposure to the harsh sun of the southern plains, he appeared to have been in his early thirties. A trickle of blood ran out of one corner of his mouth, already starting to clot in the end of an unruly ginger mustache.

Lex took a deep breath, stared once more toward the northeast. But the killers were out of sight, vanished as completely as if they had never been. If it hadn't been for the bloody corpse in front of him, Lex would have wondered if he was starting to hallucinate from the fever beginning to chill him all over.

Shaking his head, he got onto his knees, then hauled himself to his feet. Drawing his Colt, he walked over to the injured mare. He knelt beside it and stroked its muzzle. "There, there," he said.

After getting up again, he put the horse out of its misery. The mare quivered for a moment, then lay still. The crack of the Colt seemed to echo, even though there was nothing for miles, and he realized he was hearing the sound in his own head, slowly dwindling away to nothing.

He turned then, holstered the Colt, and stood looking at the dead man. He had nothing with which to bury him, and couldn't bring himself to leave the body for the buzzards already beginning to circle overhead, their massive wings motionless on the sun-whitened air. He tilted his head, measuring the big man for weight, wondering how he was going to get the body up onto the bay.

It wouldn't get any easier if he waited, so he walked to the bay, snagged the reins, and tugged the horse toward the dead man. The bay was a little skittish. There was too much death in the air, too much blood. The bay held still while he knelt to hoist the dead man, who was lighter than he looked. Getting the body over his shoulder, he could smell the blood, the stink of voided bowels, and tried to hold his breath. After draping the limp carcass over the bay, he leaned against the horse for a moment as little spurts of light flashed before his eyes, small globes hung at the edges of his field of vision.

Swallowing hard, he took his lariat and lashed the body over the big bay's rump, then climbed into the saddle while he could still move. Nudging the bay with his knees, he headed back toward the trail.

It was an hour before the first hint of Laidlaw came into view, a solitary roofline hovering on the horizon like the hull of a dismasted ship, a slightly angled shadow in the bright sun. It was another hour before he reached the edge of the town. The dusty streets looked as if they had been overbaked, then covered with brown flour. The buildings looked deserted. The dozen or so horses hitched along the main street looked as if they had been stuffed and mounted. Only the switch of their tails suggested otherwise. It was the only movement in the silent streets.

Lex rode down the center, the town beginning to dissolve before his eyes, the timber turning to water.

"Howdy," someone said, and he turned toward the voice. An old man, his full beard as yellow as it was white, flashed him a nearly toothless grin, then stepped forward to catch him as he fell from the saddle.

LEX felt something pulling at him and tried to open his eyes. The pressure under his arms was lifting him, but a stab of pain through his left shoulder pushed him back down into a deep, black well, and the light was gone almost as suddenly as it had come.

He could hear voices, but they were far away and indistinct. He was floating, and he tried desperately to open his eyes. The voices faded in and out, sometimes sounding as if they were coming from someplace right behind him, then going away again, faint echoes that he knew he should be able to understand, if only the people would come closer.

His ears rang, and his head felt as if it were spinning. He couldn't feel his body anymore, not even the pain in his left shoulder. Everything was wrapped in something thick and soft, like the old comforter full of goose down his grandmother had given him so long ago. He tried to visualize her. Something, he thought it must be a face, started to materialize in the distance, and he tried to move toward it. It floated, silent as a hawk high in the sky, but the harder he tried, the more helpless he felt.

Then for one moment the blurred face sped toward him. It stopped for a split second, and he tried to reach out for it. It still was indistinct, like the face of a woman wearing a dark veil. He could feel his slack muscles trying to move his hands to lift the veil, but he was powerless to do anything. It was a woman, though; he was sure of that. Her hands appeared, one on either side of her face, and lifted the veil, slowly, as if teasing him.

The face grew brighter, more distinct, and he screamed, could feel the tearing in his throat, but there was no sound. The woman smiled, and he knew he had seen her before, but couldn't find her name. It was buried somewhere deep inside him. He tried to roll his head from side to side, trying to shake the name loose, but it wouldn't come. Then it was gone, as abruptly as a candle extinguished by the wind.

Once more he tried to scream. His throat burned with the effort, but he knew he hadn't made a sound, and then her name came to him—Rosalita—and he slipped away, falling deeper and deeper into the darkness, the echo of one last silent scream lingering in the blackness.

When he awoke, he felt as if he were on fire. His eyes

darted from corner to corner, trying to place the room. The stark walls were unfamiliar. They could have been anywhere. A block of sunlight, tilted into a parallelogram leaning toward the right, where he saw a door, was too bright for him to look at, and he hooded his eyes, trying to take in the room. No matter how he tried to shield his eyes, the brilliant light seemed to sear them, blur their vision.

He tried to sit up, but his body ignored the impulse. His fingers felt the sheets tangled around him, damp, clammy cloth, and he was too weak even to move his legs to free them. His arms wouldn't move, either. Once more he tried to sit, but the effort took what little strength he had, and he slipped back into unconsciousness.

The next time he woke, the room was dark. He could barely make out the walls, pitch black in the dark gray space. Still too weak to sit up, he concentrated on trying to see and hear. Somewhere in the distance he thought he heard a piano, but when he tried to focus his attention on the sound, it stopped. As his eyes adjusted to the gloom, he could make out faint shapes on either side of him. They seemed to hover a few feet away, gray slabs floating motionlessly. It took him a moment to realize they were beds, at least one on either side. He must be in a ward of some kind, he thought. Maybe a hospital or a medical clinic.

He tried to call out, but his throat was too dry. He managed a faint croak, unintelligible even to himself, and he wasn't sure what it was he had tried to say. The sheets were still damp, and he tried to recall what had happened to him, why he might be here. He felt the pain in his shoulder then for the first time, and he groaned.

He could turn his head, and his right arm moved a little, although so slowly he felt foolish. His hand crept up over his right hip, a brittle crab climbing out of the sea. He could feel the weight of the hand on his hip, then his stomach. The sheet stopped halfway up, its dampness replaced by dry skin, his fingers rasping over his chest. Lex could feel the heat of his body under his fingers. Fever, for sure—how high and how long he could only guess.

When his hand reached his chin, he felt whiskers— three, maybe four days' growth. The skin beneath them was stiff, as if it had been burned by the sun, but that couldn't be. The fever must have parched him, shriveled him like an abandoned corn husk. The scrape of his fingertips over the stiff beard was like distant thunder, and even that little effort made his head swim.

Turning his head to one side, he felt something cool and damp, a folded cloth, probably a compress. It took him nearly a minute to reach it with the slowly creeping hand, and he tugged it back onto his forehead. He noticed a gray mass, curtains he thought, against the wall behind his bed. They didn't move. Either the window was closed or the hushed air outside was perfectly still.

He could hear the piano again, very faintly, a tune he'd heard before. He tried to shape its words in his mind, but they were too slippery for him. He saw something else, next to the bed—a small table and what must be a pitcher of water, its faint shape too round, too regular to be his imagination. He desperately wanted a drink, but knew he didn't have the strength to reach the table.

He heard something else then. Creaking, like that of boards under weight, someone walking, but he couldn't tell where, or even if it was on the same floor or in the same building. Then footsteps thudded and the creaking grew louder. He heard a scraping sound, like carpet slippers on raw wood, and once more he tried to visualize his grandmother's face. She had worn carpet slippers the winter he had pneumonia, tending him all night for three weeks. But his grandmother was long dead, buried a thousand miles away.

Who could it be? Who was coming to tend him this time? Or was it all his imagination?

The steps grew louder, and he rolled his head back to the right. Under the door he could see a band of light, faint and very thin. It seemed to flicker, as if there were a fire beyond the door. He watched the light grow a little brighter, then start to fade a bit as the steps grew still louder, their rhythm steady, even inexorable as they drew closer and closer and closer.

Then the door creaked. A lamp hung there at the end of an arm. Beyond it, a bulky figure in flannel, supported by thick legs, the feet encased in battered carpet slippers. So, he thought, at least I was right about that. The lamp entered the room, and the figure assumed shape as his eyes adjusted. A man, a big man, over two hundred pounds, round as a barrel, his stomach straining at a checkered flannel robe.

The man came closer, lifted a chair from the foot of the bed and moved along the left side as Lex rolled his head that way, trying to see. The man had whiskers, a full white beard. Chubby cheeks, painted orange by the low flame of the lamp, bulged out on either side of a strong nose.

The man set the lamp on the table. Lex could see the pitcher clearly now, and a glass tumbler beside it, its bottom up. The glass rotated in the man's thick fingers, and Lex heard the splash of water, saw the thin stream, like liquid gold, slowly fill the tumbler.

The man looked at him closely then. Lex tried to speak, but his tongue was too thick and too dry. The shapeless words fell short, stumbling over fever-numbed lips and falling meaninglessly to the pillow beside his head.

"You're awake, eh, partner?" the man said. His voice was deep, had a faint accent, probably German. One slablike hand reached out for Lex, rested heavily on his forehead for several moments.

The man shook his head. "High fever, very high. Not good."

He reached for the full tumbler with one hand and slid the other under Lex's head. Bringing the tumbler close, shifting it in his grasp before letting its rolled edge rest on the parched skin of Lex's lower lip, he mumbled, "*Trinken sie, bitte. Trinken sie.*"

Lex tried. His lips felt as if they had been welded

together. He felt the water well out over them, then trickle down his cheek. The pillowcase grew damp and cool beside his left ear. He tried to swallow, felt some water make its way down his throat. Frustrated, he tried yet again to swallow, but it was almost impossible.

The man, sensing the difficulty, took the tumbler away. "Wait a bit," he said. "It'll get easier."

Lex nodded, a movement so slight he thought the man might not notice it. He nodded again, and the thick hand descended to his forehead once more. "Save your strength, partner. You don't have much left."

Lex groaned. Moving his lips as if they might shatter, he said, "Water..."

The big man nodded. "Sure thing," he said. "But take it slow. Real slow." He reached for the tumbler, found it without looking, and brought it back to Lex's lips. Tilting it carefully, he let Lex suck at the rim of the glass, taking in only as much as he could handle. His throat was beginning to loosen a little, and his mouth no longer felt as if it had been carved out of year-old corncobs. Even his tongue seemed to move more freely.

The big man took the tumbler away and set it on the table again. He stood up, groaning, then reached down, snatched the compress from Lex's forehead, and said, "I'll be right back."

Lex watched the big man leave, listening to the hiss and slap of the carpet slippers on the floor. After the man had disappeared through the doorway, Lex turned his head from side to side taking in his surroundings. He was lying in the middle one of three beds. The other two were made up, their blankets drawn taut enough to balance a double eagle on edge.

The room was clean and sparsely furnished. Another small table stood to the right, an upended pitcher and glass on a white cloth. It seemed to be some sort of clinic or small hospital. A couple of chairs and a single armoire were the only other furnishings. The door of the armoire was open, and Lex saw his gun belt hanging from a peg. His hat was on a second peg, pants and shirt folded and lying on the bottom shelf. They looked as if they had been cleaned.

How long had he been out? Lex wondered. He looked around for a calendar, but saw nothing, not even a clock, to mark the passage of hours, let alone days. He could hear the slippers again, and a moment later the big man reappeared in the doorway.

The compress, newly dampened, had been refolded and rested on one large palm held flat like a small tray. The man crossed the room, leaned over, and shaped the compress to Lex's forehead. The cool cloth seemed to drain away the last of his energy, and Lex closed his eyes.

"That's right, partner," the big man said, "*schlaffen Sie.*"

Lex was too tired to answer. Through his fevered eyelids, he was aware of the light growing dimmer. Then he heard the door close.

He slept.

IT was morning when Lex awoke again. This time he knew immediately where he was. He was still hot, but the fever seemed to have broken. Brilliant sunlight streamed through the window, its harshness softened only a little by the gauzy curtain. He was still weak, but managed to reach the water pitcher and tumbler. One by one, he brought them to the mattress and, balancing the glass on the edge of the bed, managed to pour himself a drink.

Still parched by the fever, his lips were cracked, and it hurt to move them, but he had to have a drink. He remembered the big man who had tended to him the night before, or was it two nights ago? He wasn't sure. His watch must be in the pocket of his jeans, he thought, but there was just no way he could get to it.

He'd have to wait until the big man came back. But how long?

Lex drank the glass of water, poured himself another, then set the drink on the floor while he replaced the pitcher on the small night table. Raising the glass again, he emptied half of it, then lay back, balancing the tumbler on his chest. The glass felt cool to his fevered skin, and he moved it through the hair on his chest, still damp with sweat.

His left arm hurt like hell. Every time he moved, a shooting pain stabbed through the shoulder, as if someone had slammed him with a hammer. For a few seconds he could feel his pulse pounding away, sending another dozen small tongues of flame licking along the bone.

Finishing the water, he examined the room more closely. It was no less sparely furnished than he remembered, but at least he could see things clearly now. Few details caught his eye. Neat and clean, the room was also Spartan. But everything was in decent condition, the furniture even sparkling a little, as if it had been recently oiled.

The smell of the room was vaguely familiar, but Lex couldn't quite place it. He was still groggy, and his eyes went out of focus every time he moved his head. It took a few seconds for them to refocus, and the intervening seconds were not unlike having dived into a pool of crystal clear water with opened eyes. He knew things were there, but didn't see them well enough to identify them.

The building seemed to be perfectly silent. No sound came from below that he could hear. There was noise in the street. He heard the creak of a wagon, its bed twisting as it negotiated ruts in the center of town. Some distance away, he could hear what sounded like conversation, but the voices were too indistinct for him to hear what was being said.

He heard a shout, somebody snapping at a child, he thought. It sounded like a woman's voice, a little husky, but still with that softness around the edges.

Then a door slammed, and the window beside the bed rattled. He heard footsteps then, but not the scrape of the carpet slippers he remembered. The tread was lighter as it mounted the stairs. A second later the door swung open. A woman stood there, a tray in one hand, the other hand just falling away from the doorknob.

She was on the tall side, maybe five-six or a little more. Blond hair hung straight over her shoulders, long and shiny, as if it had just been washed. Her figure was slender, but not unattractively so. She wore a faded blue shirt, two buttons undone at the top, and faded jeans, threadbare patches of white bearing testimony to hard wear. They fit her long legs snugly, and he noticed the play of muscles in her thighs as she approached the bed.

She smiled, apparently something she did easily and often.

"Daddy said you might be awake," she told him, flashing another smile and stepping gracefully around the foot of the bed. She balanced the tray easily as she crossed the floor.

"Daddy?"

"That's right, you haven't really met, have you?"

"He the man who was tending to me?"

"For four days. But that's his way. Sometimes I think being a doctor is the only thing keeps him going." She set the tray on the night table, using its edge to move the pitcher to make room.

"Four days, did you say? What's today?"

"Tuesday. July sixteenth."

Lex rolled his head from side to side. She wasn't looking at him, but must have heard the movement, because she said, "I know. It's always like that. You don't realize how fast it goes by until you're unconscious, or damned near, for a few days. Seems like a big hunk of your life then."

She had the tray arranged to her satisfaction now, and turned to look at him. "I'm Anna," she said, extending one tanned hand. "Anna Kraus."

"And you say your father's been tending me?"

She nodded. "Dr. Henry Kraus. Actually, it's Heinrich, but that seems too German to him, so he prefers Henry. I can really get his goat if I call him Heinrich or, worse yet, Heinie. He hates that."

"You get his goat often?"

"Often as I have to. He's a man, after all. They usually

need to be kept in line. I expect you're no different. Whoever you are."

Lex felt embarrassed. "Cranshaw. Lex Cranshaw. Sorry, I didn't—"

"That's all right. You've been through a lot. Can't really expect manners soon as you wake up, can we?"

"Still..."

"Breeding. I smell breeding, Mr. Cranshaw. Either that or you been reading too many newspaper stories about the fabled southern gentility."

Lex laughed for a moment, but the pain cut it short. When the pain subsided, he said, "It must be the newspapers. It sure as hell ain't breeding."

"You up to a little breakfast? Not much, because it's too soon, but Doc... Daddy—everybody else calls him Doc, so I slip once in a while—says you ought to get something down if you can."

Lex tried to sit up, but he was still too weak. Anna pressed him back to the mattress with a hand that was surprisingly strong. "Wait," she said. "I'll get you up in a moment." She poured coffee from a small pot, then looked at him out of the corner of her eye. "Sugar?" she asked.

He shook his head. "Black," he said.

Anna Kraus went to a corner closet he hadn't noticed and came back with a bed chair, little more than a back and arms, well padded and shaped vaguely like the upper half of an easy chair. Lex tried to get up again as she walked toward him, and Anna snapped, "Wait a minute, Mr. Cranshaw. I told you I'd help you."

She leaned over him, and he noticed her scent for the first time—powder, with a little something, flowery but not overpowering. She smelled freshly scrubbed. As she leaned forward, he noticed the handful of freckles on her chest where the blue work shirt gaped a little. He could see the sunburned V edged in creamy white where the freckles were more prominent.

Her face was prettier than he had realized, a fact disguised by the absence of makeup of any kind. Eyes as blue as a summer sky were crinkled at the outer corners, further evidence of the ease with which she smiled. Her nose was small and turned up, her lips full, especially the lower, which looked almost bee-stung in its fleshiness.

Working the bed seat in behind him, she handled his head and upper body without apparent strain. When she was satisfied, she stepped back, then reached for the tray and lowered it across the arms of the bed seat.

"I'd better handle the coffee," she said. "It's hot, and you're in no shape to be exerting yourself too much. I'll feed you, too, if you like."

Lex bristled. "I can take care of myself, Miss Kraus."

She nodded, a trace of a mocking smile turning up the corners of her mouth. "Of course you can. That's why you're here, isn't it?"

"The hell I . . ."

He shook his head then, realizing just how feeble his protest must seem to her. "I'm sorry," he said, "it's just that I—"

"You're not used to being taken care of. It makes you feel vulnerable and just a little too much like a child. That's always the way. The tougher the man, the worse he takes it."

"You talk as if you've seen a lot of that."

"More than I care to," she said, but did not explain further.

Lex took the fork from the tray and used its edge to slice through a layer of flapjacks, cutting a neat wedge. He speared it, and lifted it carefully, waiting until the excess syrup had drained off before moving it toward his mouth.

"You're very neat, Mr. Cranshaw. That must mean you are married."

"Why is that?"

"Because most single men are a little sloppy. Syrup on the sheet is not a problem for them. Cigarette burns in the pillow, dust under the bed, dirt under the fingernails. It all goes together."

"You're wrong."

"No, I'm not."

Lex saw Rosalita for just an instant. He hadn't thought of her for ... he didn't know how long. Not long, really. He remembered thinking about her on the ride into Laidlaw, the fever already swelling his brain, making him a little loco, calling up old memories, old pains. But he was unwilling to give the smug Miss Anna Kraus the satisfaction of knowing just how close to being right she had come.

"May I have some coffee, please?"

She said nothing. Lifting the cup from the table, she brought it toward him, flinching a bit when he closed his hands around hers to tilt the cup a little and suck at the coffee.

"Sorry," he said, after swallowing a scalding mouthful. It hurt going down, but letting her know that would have been another small defeat, so he tried to disguise the pain.

Nodding his head, he waited for her to withdraw the cup, then let go of her hand. Picking up the fork again, he cut three more wedges from the pancakes, chewed each one just enough to make it easy to swallow, then lay back, feeling strangely winded, as if the energy of chewing had been more exhausting than climbing stairs under a sack of flour.

"They're very good," he said.

"I didn't make them."

Lex nodded. "Still, they're very good."

This time she said nothing. When she sensed he wanted more coffee, she handed him the cup, as if unwilling to feel his hands a second time.

Lex noticed, but didn't comment.

"The sheriff will be around to see you later this afternoon," she said.

He almost asked why, then realized with a shock that he had forgotten the dead farmer. He nodded then. "Of course," he said.

"If you're not up to it, Daddy can tell him to wait until tomorrow."

"I've never yet met a lawman who gave a tinker's

damn for what a sawbones said."

"You have a lot of experience with lawmen, Mr. Cranshaw?"

"Some," he said.

LEX was sitting up in bed when the sheriff arrived. He'd heard the clomp of boots on the stairs, and was looking toward the door. A big man, nearly two hundred pounds, the sheriff was sunburned, his ginger mustache needing a trim, its scraggly ends sun-bleached almost white. His large hands looked to be mostly knuckle. The thick fingers moved stiffly, like frozen snakes just beginning to thaw.

"How you feeling, Cranshaw?" he asked.

"I been better, Sheriff."

"Name's Pete Cannon. Doc Kraus said he dug a bullet out of your shoulder, that right?"

Lex smiled. "Hard to tell. It still feels like hell. But I could believe somebody dug something out of it."

The sheriff didn't smile back. "You mind tellin' me how you come to stop a bullet?"

"Not as fast as I used to be, I guess."

Cannon pushed his hat back and lowered himself to a chair. "Let me stop you right there, Cranshaw. This just ain't a laughing matter. Look at it from my point of view. Fellow I never seen before rides into my town half dead. He's got a dead man where his bedroll ought to be. The dead man I know. You I don't. Now, you see anything funny there? 'Cause if you do, then you and me got to talk about your sense of humor."

Lex nodded. "You're right, Sheriff. I'm sorry. I guess I'm just a little off kilter. The doc is giving me some medicine—laudanum, I think—and..."

"I'll accept that. I got no quarrel with you, least none that I know of. But I got a lot of questions. And I expect you to have a lot of answers."

"Go ahead, Sheriff. Ask."

"You know Gunther, did you?"

"That his name?"

Cannon nodded. "Gunther Kleinhalder. Pretty new around here, less than a year. Has... had a small spread outside town a few miles. Left a wife and a couple of kids. I'd like to know what happened."

"Never saw him before the day I came in here."

"Tell me all about it. Right from the beginning. I want to know everything. Don't leave nothing out."

Lex did. It took him ten minutes, and when he was done, his mouth was dry as dust. He reached for the pitcher and a glass, poured himself some water, and took a long swallow.

"Cranshaw, let me ask you something. How'd you come to get yourself shot?"

"My partner and I were down south of the Nueces. Tracking a wanted man, three murders that we knew of and probably as many more we didn't know about."

"Tracking, what do you mean? You bounty hunters or something?"

"Jace and me are... Texas Rangers. I thought I mentioned that. I guess my old guitar is a little more loosely strung than I thought. Sorry."

"Ranger, huh? And where's your partner?"

"Dead. So's Cord Schuster, the man we were tracking. I was heading back to Austin when I ran across Kleinhalder. I wish to hell I'd been in better shape. Maybe I could have done something."

Cannon sucked on a tooth. "You get a look at the men done the shooting?"

Lex, puzzled that Cannon had not asked about Schuster and Jace, took his time before answering. When he did, he chose his words carefully. Even through the medicinal fog that clouded his brain, he could sense something odd about the sheriff's approach. "No," he said, shaking his head. "Never got halfway close enough."

"Would you recognize any of 'em if you seen 'em again?"

"Not a chance, Sheriff. I wish I could help you, but... You have any idea who might have done it?"

"None at all, Cranshaw. None at all. I was kinda hoping you could give me something to chew on. As it is, there ain't very much to work with."

"They didn't take anything. Never even got off their horses or looked at the body to make sure Kleinhalder was dead. They knew it. So I don't think it was a robbery."

"You didn't give 'em a chance, did you? I mean, a man comes riding down on me like you say you done, guns blazing and alla that, I reckon I might leave in a hurry, too."

It sounded nice, but it was too pat. They were three to his one, and he was wounded. It seemed to Lex, now that he thought about it, that they were interested in just one thing, and they managed to do it with about as little fuss as possible. But Lex kept the thought to himself. "I guess you're right."

"You want me to get in touch with anybody? You expected somewhere?"

"You could send a telegram to Austin for me, if you would. Major Earl Podell. Just tell him I've been wounded. I'll write him a letter later. Tell him that, too."

"That all?"

Lex shrugged. "No point to anything else. You got any idea who might have had it in for Kleinhalder?"

"Didn't know him well enough to be sure, but not as far as I know."

"It was cold, Sheriff, I'll tell you that much. Whoever killed him didn't give a damn about him. I've seen people show more compassion to a rattlesnake."

"It's not your problem, Cranshaw. Don't let it trouble you none. We'll find whoever done it, and we'll deal with them. It'll take a while, maybe, but we'll get 'em."

Lex shifted his shoulders to ease the pain a little. If Cannon noticed, it didn't seem to bother him. "You'll probably want me to stay around as a witness."

"No need. You claim you didn't see much. What kind of witness would you be?"

"I'm the only one saw anything. I'm the only witness you got, Sheriff."

"And what you saw was nothing at all. That don't make you much of a witness. Like I said, we'll handle it. Soon as you can ride, you might as well go on back to Austin or wherever it is you was heading."

Cannon stood up, adjusted his gun belt, and yawned. "Might as well head on back to the office," he said. "You think of anything else, you let me know. And when you're ready to leave town, you drop by and leave word where I can reach you, in case I need to."

"I won't be leaving Laidlaw for at least two or three days," Lex said.

Cannon nodded. "All right," he said. "I'll see you before then." He walked to the door, turned in the doorway, and leaned one shoulder against the doorframe. "You ain't holding back anything, are you, Cranshaw?"

"Now, Sheriff, why would I do that?"

"Just so you don't." And he was gone.

Lex lay there, wondering what it was about the sheriff that disturbed him. The man seemed curiously detached from the murder of Gunther Kleinhalder, but lawmen were often like that. They got to see men at their worst, and for some, the best way to deal with the ugliness was to turn off their feelings. Lex understood it, but he didn't like it. He couldn't do it himself, and often wondered whether it made him better or worse than those who could.

But there had been an undercurrent to Cannon's questions. He wasn't talking lawman to lawman, more like lawman to suspect. Lex wondered whether Cannon suspected him of having had more to do with the shooting than he was saying. Or was Cannon thinking about something else entirely, he wondered. Lex didn't like feeling like a suspect, and he wasn't sure he liked Cannon's attitude. But he'd have to mull it over before he could put his finger on the reasons.

He lay back and closed his eyes, letting the questions whirl in his head, high and distant, silent as buzzards. He was still weak, and his shoulder throbbed painfully, but at least the fever was down, almost gone altogether. Now it was just a question of getting his strength back. He took a deep breath, then let it out slowly, listening to the hammering of blood in his ears, feeling every heartbeat poke its tiny white-hot knife into his shoulder.

He felt the hand on his forehead then and snapped his eyes open.

"It's just me," Anna Kraus said. "Why are you so nervous, Mr. Cranshaw?"

Lex shrugged his shoulders, then winced. "I didn't hear you come in."

"It's a habit I have." She smiled distantly, as if at a memory instead of him. "When you've tended to as many sick and wounded as I have, you learn to be quiet. Angel of mercy and all that."

Lex scraped a tentative hand over his whiskers. For a moment the rasp of skin on bristle was the only sound in the room.

"Would you like me to shave you?" Anna asked.

"I can handle it, Miss Kraus."

She shook her head. "No, you can't, Mr. Cranshaw. Your hands aren't steady enough. You'd end up bleeding to death. And then I'd have to clean the sheets. I'll take care of it."

She turned and left before he could argue with her. Ten minutes later she was back once more, a tray balanced on one hand. When she set it on the edge of the bed, he saw a bowl of hot water, little wisps of steam circling above it, a mug of soap, a shaving brush, and a straight razor. Over one arm she had draped a towel.

After dipping the brush into the hot water, she worked up a thick wad of foam in the mug. Swirling the brush to thicken the foam a bit more, she watched him closely. He felt her eyes on him, lingering on his face, evaluating him, and he waited for her to say whatever she was thinking. Instead, she started to slap the lather onto his cheeks, pushed his head back with the heel of her free hand, and worked the foam under his chin and down his neck. The lather was hot, but it felt good and he bit his tongue rather than complain.

When his face was covered, he closed his eyes and leaned back. He felt the touch of the cold steel on one cheek and heard the first scrape of the razor.

"What do you think of our Sheriff Cannon?" she finally asked.

"I'm not sure. Why?"

"Just curious."

"No, it's more than that. What's on your mind?"

"Nothing."

He started to argue, but she pressed her free hand over his mouth, forcing a little soap between his lips. "Hold still," she said. "You'll get cut."

The room was filled with the scratch of steel on whisker. As the hair and thick foam came away from his cheeks, he could feel the warm air on his skin. He realized that he hadn't felt really clean for weeks. Anna said not another word. She moved his head about to get at the crevices under his nose, pulled the skin taut to get the jawbone smooth, then wrapped his face in a hot towel.

Lying there, swathed like a mummy, his eyes closed while the warmth soaked into him, he was beginning to feel whole again.

"He's scum," Anna said.

LEX was getting his strength back, and he was tired of lying around feeling like an invalid. He swung his legs over the side of the bed and stood up. His head spun a bit, but he closed his eyes until the vertigo passed. Standing there in the dark, he could feel his body swaying, as if the slightest breeze through the open window would knock him off his feet. Even in the dark, it was better to keep his eyes closed to ward off the dizziness that threatened to sweep him away.

Reaching down with his left hand, he felt for the edge of the mattress, then moved toward the wall until he could touch the night table. Opening his eyes again, he looked at the curtains swaying in the night air. The filmy cotton picked up the moonlight and seemed to shimmer, the way a darting fish under clear water will pick up sunlight just an instant before it vanishes.

Bracing himself on the table, he moved closer to the window. Leaning on the sill, he pulled the gauze curtain aside and lowered himself to his knees. Leaning out the window, he could feel the hot breath of night wind on his cheeks. It felt for a moment like the flush of a returning fever, but he adjusted quickly and looked down into the deserted streets of Laidlaw, the shadows of the buildings silent and dark where they spilled into the road.

The dirt of the street, rutted by wagon wheels, was striped where shadow filled the wheel tracks. Everything looked as if it were made of metal or plated with tarnished silver. Even the clods and clumps of dirt kicked up by hooves looked like fist-sized nuggets. Up the block he could hear a piano, out of tune, being hammered by someone with more energy than finesse. The tune, if there was one, was not one he recognized.

He wanted to go outside, take the air, suck a little life back into his body, maybe even have a drink. Doc Kraus wouldn't approve, and he could already hear Anna's scolding, see a finger shaken in his face as she lectured him for being too concerned with a man's stupid sense of his own vulnerability. And Anna would be right, he thought. It was so easy to fall into a trap like that. He'd done his share of it. But what Anna Kraus didn't understand was that image was sometimes all a man had. If he was unsure of himself, he had to push a little, test himself, find out what his limits were. It was foolish, maybe, but better than living with uncertainty. There was enough of that in a man's life already.

He backed away from the window and got up slowly. This time, there was no dizziness, and he was starting to feel a little more in control, a little less vulnerable. He moved back to the night table and groped for the drawer pull, opened the small drawer and felt around in the blackness until he found a small box of wooden matches.

After opening the box, he removed a match, struck it, and reached for the glass chimney of a small lamp on the table. He lit the wick, adjusted it once until the flame caught, then replaced the chimney. His hands, he noticed, were shaking a little, but he ignored the tremors and walked to the armoire, aware of the orange glow brightening a little as the coal oil settled into a steady flame.

He opened the armoire, then paused for a moment until his eyes adjusted to the gloom, found his clothes and gun belt, and walked back to the bed. After sitting on the foot of the mattress, he set his clothes to one side and pulled his Colt from its holster. He broke the cylinder and hefted the Colt for a moment, trying to remember the last time he had gone so many days without a gun in his hand.

Tilting the Colt, he shook it and caught the shells in his open palm. Four were empty, the fifth was a live round. The sixth was still in the cylinder, and he slid a fingernail under the rim of the cartridge and pulled it free. It, too, was an empty round.

He moved closer to the lamp, ignoring his clothes

when they slid off the mattress and landed on the floor. The Colt was dusty, but his cleaning kit was in his saddlebags, stuffed in the bottom of the armoire. Leaning toward the flickering lamp, he blew dust out of the cylinder, then realized the gun had to be cleaned and oiled. He set it on the mattress and stood up. Once more, his body, its equilibrium disrupted by the sudden movement, rebelled. He waited until the dizziness passed, then retrieved the saddlebags.

He opened one bag and found the small pouch with its vial of gun oil, the oily rags, and a tool kit. Unwilling to soil the bedcovers, and even less willing to confront Anna Kraus if she realized what he had been up to, which she surely would if he got oil on the covers, he sat on the floor, the heavy Colt in his lap.

His life depended on his weapons, and he knew the Colt better than he knew his own body. He worked smoothly, cleaning the gun, wiping it free of sand and grit, oiling it, then wiping away the excess gun oil in a mindless fashion, letting his instincts and his years of practice guide him. He could do it in the dark, and had done so more than once.

When the Colt was clean, and the room full of the sharp tang of the oil, he got to his knees and reached for the gun belt. He loaded the one remaining good round, then popped five more cartridges from the gun belt and slid them one after another into the black holes of the cylinder, spun it once to make sure it turned freely, then clicked it closed.

After holstering the pistol, he tossed the gun belt onto

the bed, then realized he ought to replace the cartridges on it, and got a box of .45 shells from the saddlebags. He slipped the cleaning gear back into its pouch, shoved the pouch back into the saddlebags, then loaded the gun belt until every loop held a shell.

Only then did he feel finished. Knowing the Colt was in working order gave him an odd sense of security. The single thing on which he most depended was ready once more, in case he needed it. And something told him he would need it badly before he saw the last of Laidlaw.

Anna's opinion of Pete Cannon had been bothering him. She had refused to talk about it, even when he tried to draw her out. There seemed to be more to her attitude than simple dislike, but without a clue, all he had to go on was the vague suspicion that Cannon was not what he seemed. He planned to ask Doc Kraus about it, but hadn't seen him since the previous day.

He slipped into his shirt, wincing when he flexed his wounded shoulder too quickly, then sat on the edge of the bed. Taking several deep breaths, he waited for the pain to subside before pulling his pants on.

As he tucked his shirt in, he shifted his weight on the bed, then stopped when he heard a creak on the stairs outside his door. Puzzled, he walked to the door and listened intently. The creaking had stopped. He wondered whether he had imagined it.

It was too late at night for it to be Anna or Doc Kraus. It was unlikely the sheriff would be coming to pay him a second visit at that hour. He was about to back away from the door when he heard a thud, as if someone unfamiliar with the stairs was maneuvering in the dark.

Lex tiptoed back to the bed, grabbed the Colt, and then moved to the night table, where he lifted the chimney and extinguished the lamp.

Listening again, he heard nothing. As he edged back toward the door, he was glad that he had not put his boots on. If there was an intruder, and if he had heard Lex's tread on the floor he would probably have spooked. If someone was out there, Lex wanted to know who and, especially, why.

He positioned himself between the doorframe and the armoire, flattening his back against the wall. He reached out, found the doorframe with his fingertips, and slid a little closer to the door. He held the gun high over his head, his thumb resting on the hammer, but not yet cocking it. He took a deep breath and held it.

Letting his free hand rest on the knob, he waited to see whether it would turn. Another thump, this one close, as if someone was just behind him, separated from him only by the thin wall. Lex held his breath, trying to ignore the throb in his shoulder. The tension was pulling his muscles taut, and his wounded shoulder protested the only way it knew how, by catching fire and searing the meat right down to the bone.

Then the doorknob began to turn. He let it glide under his fingers, not wanting even the slightest pressure to tip off the intruder that he had been warned.

The knob turned, and Lex let his hand fall away. The door swung open, and Lex steeled himself, but no one entered. He heard a hammer being thumbed back and cocked his Colt in response. A second later the room exploded. Two bright flashes, almost blinding in their suddenness, and two claps of thunder—a shotgun.

Lex waited, then heard footsteps moving away from the door. He moved toward the doorway and started out, bumped his bad shoulder and let out a groan. The footsteps stopped, and then started back up the stairs.

Lex held his position, waiting for the gunman to reach the top of the stairwell before showing himself.

Down below, a voice whispered hoarsely. "I thought you said you got him, Donny. Dammit."

"I did. I—"

The voice was directly in front of the doorway now, and Lex jabbed his Colt through, found ribs, and dug the barrel in a little deeper. "Hold it right there, Donny," Lex said, keeping his voice low.

He felt the movement but couldn't see anything. The sharp impact of metal on bone brought a gasp from the gunman as his wrist slammed into the Colt and shoved the gun away. Lex almost lost his grip on the pistol, swung it back, and fired once.

Someone groaned, and he heard the hoarse voice below shouting, "Donny, Donny, what's going on?"

Then the gunman fell, landing hard on the top steps.

Something clattered down the stairs. Probably the shotgun, Lex guessed.

He dropped to his knees and crawled through the doorway. Below, dimly outlined against an open doorway, he saw the shadowy figure of a cowboy, a Winchester carbine in his hand.

Once more the hoarse voice called up the stairs, "Donny, you all right?"

"Donny's in big trouble," Lex said, "and so are you."

"Shit!"

The cowboy swung the Winchester up and fired. The bullet spanged off the wall, scattering splinters in every direction, and the cowboy was gone.

Lex groped forward, found the wounded man, and crept past him, then started down the stairs. By the time he reached the ground floor, his shoulder was pounding. His head was spinning, and he staggered toward the open front door.

He heard movement behind him, heard a knob rattle, then a door swing open.

"What the hell's going on out there?" a voice bellowed. It was Doc Kraus.

"It's me, Doc."

"Cranshaw, dammit, what are you doing out of bed? Why in hell are you shooting guns at this time of night?"

"Stay where you are, Doc."

Lex groped toward the open front door and peered

cautiously into the street. As he expected, it was empty. Surprisingly, no one seemed to have heard the gunfire. Not a curtain moved, not a window was open. It was as if the town were deserted.

6

HEINRICH Kraus appeared in the doorway with a lamp *held* over his head. The doctor's bulk filled the doorway, but Lex could hear Anna somewhere behind her father. "What happened, Daddy?" she asked. "What's going on?"

Kraus turned to quiet her. "Nothing, Anna. Go back to bed. It's nothing. Nothing." He waved a hand to keep her away from the door then. Stepping into the hallway, he pulled the door closed.

Lex leaned against the wall, panting. Kraus moved toward him, holding the lamp out ahead as if it were a talisman to ward off catastrophe. "Are you all right, Mr. Cranshaw? What happened?"

Lex shook his head and swallowed hard. "I'm all right. Someone tried to kill me."

"Who? Why?" Then, planting himself in front of Lex,

the doctor reached out with his free hand. "You're bleeding," he said. "You have opened your wound again. Let me get you upstairs."

Lex shook him off. "It's all right," he said. "I'm just winded."

"You need rest, Mr. Cranshaw. Why are you dressed? You should be in bed yet, *ja*?" Not waiting for an answer, Kraus slid one thick arm under Lex's good shoulder and started toward the stairs.

"I can make it myself, Doc," Lex said. He tried to pull free, but Kraus was too strong for him.

"Sure you can, Mr. Cranshaw. I know that. But I think what you can do and what you should do are not always the same thing, yes?"

Lex, feeling a little dizzy, caved in. "Yes," he said. "You're right."

"Then let me help you." The doctor's slippers rustled on the floor as he moved closer.

The lamp filled the stairwell with its orange light. Lex involuntarily glanced toward the head of the stairs. The only sign of the assault was one hand of the wounded gunman dangling casually over the top step, its fingers curled awkwardly, like the claws of a dead bird. So far, Kraus didn't seem to have noticed.

Lex took his time, leaning on the big man's arm as Kraus negotiated the stairs sideways, the lamp leading the way, Lex trailing along behind the doctor like the limp tail of a huge kite.

"There's a wounded man upstairs," Lex gasped. "I think he's hurt pretty bad."

"So, there's a wounded man on the stairs. We will see about him. But first things first, Mr. Cranshaw. Or do you want to tell me my business?"

Kraus shifted his body to get a better hold on the wounded Ranger and moved up the last few steps, carrying Lex as much as supporting him. Setting the lamp on the landing, he lowered Lex to the steps.

"Wait a minute," he said. Leaning over the gunman, his bulk looming over Lex like a huge boulder, he clucked to himself, then shook his head, muttering under his breath.

"How is he?" Lex asked.

"Dead," the doctor answered. "Dead as ever a doornail could be."

"Do you know him?"

"No, I don't think so." Kraus rolled the dead man out of the way, then reached down for Lex. Lifting the lantern, he got a secure grip on Lex and helped him up the last few steps. On the second floor, Lex felt more in control. He still felt weak, but managed to move on his own again and followed Kraus into the infirmary.

"His name was Donny. I heard the other man call him that. You sure you don't know him?"

"Get in bed," Kraus ordered, ignoring the question. He set the lamp down on the night table and lit the second lamp, then took his own again. "You wait right here. I need a few things. I'll send Anna up in a minute to—"

"Do you think that's a good idea?" Lex asked, canting his head toward the hallway.

"Anna has seen worse." Kraus didn't wait for an argument. Lex heard him clomp down the stairs, the carpet slippers flapping and whispering. Then a door banged below.

For several minutes the silence was perfect. Only the sound of his own breathing rasping in the dimness disturbed the quiet. Then he heard Anna's voice, the words lost as she said something to her father. He heard her on the stairs then and stared at the doorway until she appeared carrying a steaming basin of hot water on a tray and clutching gauze and fresh bandages in her hand.

"Why are you dressed?" she asked. She stopped in her tracks and glared at him. He thought for a moment she was going to stamp her foot.

"I was feeling a little better. I'm tired of being cooped up, so I was going to go outside and get some fresh air. Thought it would do me good."

"You're too weak to do anything like that. You should never have gotten out of bed."

"If I hadn't been willing to try, I'd be dead now." He pointed to the rumpled cover of his original bed. The mattress was shredded, the sheets tattered, and the headboard nicked and riddled with buckshot, probably double-O.

Anna gasped, and Lex started off the other bed, thinking she was going to drop the basin, but she recovered quickly. "Who...?"

"I was hoping to ask the man in the hall that very question, but your father tells me that's not possible."

"Donny Calloway?"

"That his name? Your father said he didn't know who he was."

"But that's ridiculous! Daddy knows him as well as—" She stopped then, confused. Lex could see the wheels turning. And now he had one more question. They seemed to be accumulating like tumbleweeds stuck on a barbed-wire fence.

"Who was he?" Lex asked.

"Oh, nobody." She moved toward him then, her motion so sudden the water sloshed over the rim of the basin and wet her jeans down the front. She didn't seem to notice, despite the curling steam rising from the faded blue cloth.

"He was somebody, Anna. We're all somebody. Even a hired gun. Who was he?"

"Just, you know, a cowboy. Nothing special about him. Just a cowboy."

"Who'd he work for?"

They both heard the tread on the stairs at the same moment. The sound was of heavy boots, not Kraus's carpet slippers, and Lex yanked his Colt free. "Get in the corner," he said.

"But—"

"Do it!" he snapped. "Now!" He got off the bed and pushed her toward the far corner of the room, then moved toward the door, cocking the Colt at the same time.

"Cranshaw?" a voice called. As it dawned on Lex who it was, Pete Cannon stepped into the room.

The sheriff saw the gun and smiled. "Spooked you, did I, Cranshaw?"

"Sort of. I already had one close call tonight, Sheriff. Didn't feel like another. Not tonight, anyhow."

"I guess I can understand that. You want to tell me what happened?"

"Actually, I was hoping you could tell me."

"Now, why would you think that, Cranshaw? Or am I missing something?"

"I think one of us is missing something, Sheriff. I just don't want it to be me."

"What's that supposed to mean?"

"It means what it means. It means somebody tried to blow my head off with a shotgun—somebody I've never met, to my knowledge—for reasons I can only guess at. I never did like guessing. And I don't mind telling you I like even less *what* I'm guessing, Mr. Cannon."

"What exactly are you guessing, Mr. Cranshaw? Or is it too much to ask that you share your suspicions with the chief peace officer of this town?"

"Not at all. What I'm guessing is that somebody thinks I know more about the murder of Gunther Kleinhalder than I actually do. Which tells me that it wasn't just an unfortunate situation where Kleinhalder was in the wrong place at the wrong time. He was killed for a reason, and if I put my finger on the reason, I'll almost certainly put my finger on the man who did it, or wanted it done."

"You're making more of this than you have to. Besides, this is my problem, not yours."

"Not anymore, Sheriff. A man shoots at me, that's *my* problem."

"All right, let's say for the moment that I agree with you. I still want to know what's going on. I got some questions, and you by God better have some answers."

"You're the sheriff."

"The dead man in the hall. Was he alone?"

"No. There was at least one man with him."

"You get a look at him?"

"Nothing more than a shadow. I couldn't identify him, if that's what you're getting at. But then, I couldn't identify the men who killed Kleinhalder, either, but that wasn't good enough for somebody. I'm going to assume it won't make any difference this time around."

"And just what exactly do you propose to do about it? Or shouldn't I ask?"

"Well, originally I was planning on going back to Austin as soon as I could make the ride."

"And now?"

"Now I think maybe I'll stay around awhile. It's kind of personal with me. A man shoots my bed full of holes, I kind of like to know who did it and why. I tend to sleep better when I can answer those questions."

"Maybe you better let me put you in the lockup. For your own good."

Lex shook his head. "No, thanks. I won't learn anything locked in a jail cell."

"Maybe not, but you'll stay alive."

Lex doubted it, but decided to play along. "Maybe

so. But I'm kind of funny about bars, Sheriff. I'd rather be on the outside looking in."

Cannon laughed. "Never met a crook who didn't feel the same way, Cranshaw. No offense."

"None taken."

"You know, folks around here are kind of clannish. They don't like strangers nosing around, even if they come from Austin."

"I'll remember that."

Cannon ran a thickly veined hand across his chin. In the pale light, the shadows made his hand look as if it had been scored by a router.

"You recognize the dead man, Sheriff?"

Cannon shook his head. "Nope. But we'll find out who he is, all right. You can count on that much, at least."

"Good to know I can count on something around here."

"Don't push it too far, though. Luck has a way of running out when you ain't lookin'."

DR. Kraus returned, a black bag tucked under one arm. He walked to the bed, then looked at Anna. "Why haven't you cut the old dressing off, Anna?"

"Not yet, Doc," Lex said. "We have to talk, first. I want to know what the hell is going on around here."

"No, no, no. No talking. First we have to look at your shoulder."

"Doc, later. I have to know what's going on here. I'm in the middle of something that might get me killed. I want to know what it is and why I'm in the middle. I think you owe me that much."

"I really don't know what you mean, Mr. Cranshaw. You're in the middle of nothing that I know about. Nothing at all. Honestly—"

"The hell you don't know, Doc. I don't mean to seem

ungrateful. You've done a lot for me, probably saved my life. But you're lying to me, both of you, and I want to know why. If you're in some kind of trouble, maybe I can help you. At least let me try."

Kraus shook his head. Lex noticed that the doctor wouldn't meet his gaze, and he turned to Anna. She folded her arms across her chest, then hugged them close, as if to ward off a chill, despite the heat of the July night. Lex started to ask her a question, but she sensed it and turned her back to him, trying to defend herself against it.

Lex exploded. "Dammit! Look at me, Anna. Talk to me. Dr. Kraus, please..."

The doctor moved to the bed and sat down heavily on the edge of the mattress.

Sensing that the doctor was weakening, Lex bored in. "Doc, I'm a peace officer. Maybe I can help. Whatever is wrong, it must be very wrong. You don't strike me as a coward, but you're scared out of your wits. I can see that, but I don't know why. I can't help if you don't tell me. And I want to help. Let me decide for myself whether there is anything I can do. I'm not interested in making things worse for you and Anna, but maybe, just maybe, I can make them better. Don't you think it's worth a chance?"

"You can't." It was Anna. "There's nothing you can do about it."

Lex bristled. "Why not?"

"You are only one man, Mr. Cranshaw. One man can't possibly—"

"Go ahead, Anna," Doc Kraus told her. "Tell him."

Anna turned to face Lex again. She took one tentative step closer, then backed up. Her arms were, if anything, wrapped more tightly about her. Her lower lip trembled, and Lex leaned closer. But she said nothing. Her face suddenly went motionless. Even the trembling lip stilled. It was as if she had become Lot's wife in an instant.

"You know who killed Gunther Kleinhalder, don't you? Both of you know." Lex took care not to make it sound like an accusation. He waited patiently, shifting his gaze to Doc Kraus, then back to Anna, then back to the physician. "You both know. Tell me, dammit!" He didn't shout, but his voice slashed the silence, hissing like a razor slicing through cheap cotton.

"Clay Schiller," the doctor said. "He didn't shoot Gunther, maybe. Probably he did not. But it was done because he wanted it done. So..."

"Who is Clay Schiller?"

"He owns the biggest ranch for three hundred miles in any direction. Half of the country is his land. He is one of the most powerful men in this part of the state. And he wants more and more and more. What he has isn't enough to satisfy him. He wants everything."

"That's what Clay Schiller owns. I want to know what he *is*."

"See, I knew you wouldn't understand," Anna snapped. "And if you don't understand, you can't help. All you'll do is make things worse. You can leave here anytime you want to, but we can't. We're trapped here. We have to stay here. This is our *home*, damn you!

How dare you pretend that you give a damn about us? You don't even know us!"

"And what do you think will happen if you don't stand up to Schiller now, while there's still time? Do you think he'll leave you alone? You think he'll take everybody's land but yours?"

"That's not what—"

"It *is* what will happen, Anna. Your father knows that. So do you, if you'll just be honest with yourself. If you're right, the man didn't stop at murder. You think you can strike a bargain with a man like that? Is that what you think? Because if it is, then you're dead wrong. What happened with Kleinhalder? Did he stand up to Schiller? I'll bet he wasn't the first, either, was he?"

He stared at Anna, waiting for an answer, but she said nothing and made no movement. She might as well have been made of stone. She seemed even to have stopped breathing. Only her eyes betrayed any hint of her agitation.

Doc Kraus came to her rescue. "No, he wasn't the first. There was a young man, Karl Schliemann. He and Anna..." The doctor choked, then sighed heavily. Lex turned to Anna, but got no explanation from her. All he got was a look of profound sorrow, tinged with hatred, partly of Clayton Schiller, but partly of Lex himself, for forcing her to remember. He didn't enjoy pressuring her. He knew what it was like to be forced to remember something so painful, but she left him no choice.

"A friend of yours?" he asked, softening his tone just a little.

Anna couldn't speak. She just nodded. She swallowed hard, as if on the verge of saying something, then shook her head.

"Mr. Cranshaw," Dr. Kraus said, his accent thickening with emotion, "Anna and Karl were..."

Lex turned to look at Anna. "Your fiancé, wasn't he?" Lex asked.

"What difference does it make now?" Anna asked. "And what would a man like you know about something like that? You're no better than Clayton Schiller."

"Anna," Kraus said, "you shouldn't talk like that. Mr. Cranshaw is just trying to help."

"We don't need his help. We don't *want* his help. Why won't he leave us alone?"

"You may not want it, Anna, but you sure as hell do need it."

"And what can you do? One man, wounded—you think you can defeat a man like Clay Schiller?"

"It looks like I'm gonna have to, Anna. The dead man, he worked for Schiller?"

She nodded.

"And Cannon? He's Schiller's man, too, isn't he? Schiller owns him somehow, doesn't he?"

"Yes, dammit! He worked for Schiller before he became sheriff. He killed the last sheriff, and then Schiller had Cannon appointed by the mayor."

Lex nodded slowly. "So they're all in Schiller's pocket. Everybody you'd turn to for help belongs to the man you need help against, is that it?"

"Yes, that's it. And that's why you don't have a

chance. That's why we won't fight, because we can't win. There's no one to turn to, and no one wants to be the next Karl Schliemann or Gunther Kleinhalder. And I don't blame them. A man would have to be a fool to—"

Lex interrupted her. "I don't want to die, either, Anna. I understand what's happened. I know how it works. I know how a man like Clay Schiller manages to get everything he wants. He probably has a bunch of hired hands who like to brawl, don't mind the smell of gun smoke or the sight of blood. Some of them probably even like it more than a little. And the good people in Laidlaw feel like they're alone. They can't count on the law, because there is no law for them. They can't count on their neighbors because each of them is used to acting alone. That's how it works. Keep everybody off balance and squash anybody who doesn't toe the mark."

"And you think you can do something about it, do you, Mr. Cranshaw?"

"I can try, Anna. Hell, I'm *paid* to try. And I always earn my money."

"Men are all alike, so full of themselves, so sure they can do anything, beat anyone. And that's where you're wrong, because you can't beat someone like Schiller."

"Maybe we shouldn't be so quick to disagree with Mr. Cranshaw, Anna. Maybe he knows what he's talking about, yes? At least we could listen to what he has to say. What could it hurt to listen?"

The doctor stood up and turned to Lex. "Maybe we

should look at your arm before we talk more." He jabbed a finger at Lex's wounded shoulder, the shirt now dark with blood oozing through the bandages. "Anna, help Mr. Cranshaw with his shirt, *bitte*."

Anna finally unclasped her arms and took a tentative step toward her father. "Yes, Daddy," she said. Then, wiping at the corner of one eye, burying one white knuckle in the soft flesh beneath the eye for a second, she sniffed back a tear and leaned toward Lex.

He started to remove the shirt. The blood had already begun to coagulate, and the cloth was sticking to the bandage beneath it. Impatient, and with just a trace of spite, Anna snatched at the shirt and jerked it roughly. Lex winced in spite of himself, and Anna, satisfied that she had hurt him a little, apologized, but didn't mean it. She knew that Lex knew it, and she didn't give a damn.

Doc Kraus snipped the blood-soaked bandage away. Lex glanced at the wound. It gaped open, and Kraus shook his head. "I think maybe I have to put in some stitches," he muttered. "Anna, get some whiskey, please." To Lex he said, "This will hurt a bit."

Lex nodded.

"Yes, Daddy," Anna said, scowling at Lex once more before leaving the room.

Kraus busied himself swabbing the open wound, wiping the blood away with a damp cloth. "I think maybe you are taking too much on yourself, Mr. Cranshaw," he whispered. "But I will do what I can to help you. Just don't get Anna involved. She is all I have. If anything were to happen to her—"

"Nothing will happen, Dr. Kraus. But I can't just walk away from this. It's not just what Schiller is doing to the people here. It's personal now."

"*Ja*, I understand, but—"

Lex cut him off. "Where is Schiller's ranch? I think maybe I'd like to pay him a little visit, try to get some idea of what I'm up against."

"You will not get to him. He has men to protect him. The place is guarded day and night. He is intent on crushing everything and everyone to get his way. He can't see that he has already won, that there is no one in Laidlaw to stand up to him any longer."

"Is there anyone you can trust? Would anyone be willing to stand up to Schiller if—"

"Sssshhh. Anna *kommt*. We talk later, yes?"

Lex nodded. "Damn right we will, Doc. Damn right we will."

LEX slept poorly. He tossed and turned half the night, more than once imagining the sound of footsteps on the stairs. But each time, after pulling his Colt and tiptoeing to the door, he yanked it open only to find the darkness outside the door silent, and the stairs empty.

By dawn, with little more than a couple of hours of sleep, mostly catnaps strung fitfully together, he was wide awake. His arm hurt from the stitches, but it no longer bled, and when he got up, he wasn't dizzy. He was already dressed and strapping on his gun belt when Anna Kraus came up the stairs carrying his breakfast.

She stepped into the room and froze for a moment. "And just what do you think you're doing, Mr. Cranshaw?" she demanded.

"Miss Kraus." He nodded. "Going to take a room at the hotel."

"Why?"

"Because I have a feeling I'll be around here for a few days yet, and I don't want to impose."

"But you're not imposing. Besides, you're still weak. You need rest, and you should stay here where my father can keep an eye on you."

Lex shook his head. "Thanks, but I think it's best if I move to the hotel. You and Dr. Kraus have been hospitable, and I thank you for your kindness, but—"

"Please, Mr. Cranshaw, don't do it."

Lex looked at the tray in her hands. "I'll have some breakfast, if I might."

"Of course."

"On one condition..."

"What?"

"That you stay and tell me everything you know about Clay Schiller."

Anna looked doubtful. She chewed on her lower lip for several moments, then nodded her head, a faint gesture of assent, so uncertain that Lex knew she wasn't sure she could do what he was asking.

"Was that a yes?" he asked.

"Yes, I suppose it was."

"I want to know everything, so don't hold back on me. No matter what it is, even if you think it's unimportant, I want you to tell me."

Lex pulled up a chair, then sat on the bed. Anna

lowered the tray onto the chair, dragged a second one over beside it, and sat down. "All right," she said.

Lex listened while he ate, occasionally asking for clarification, sometimes asking her to repeat something. When he had finished the ham, eggs, and hashbrowns, she was still talking. Lex sipped his coffee, leaning back away from the tray and watching her face closely. She didn't look at him, hadn't laid eyes on him the whole time she spoke. She almost seemed ashamed of something, as if the behavior of the town and especially her own behavior were an embarrassment, something sinful.

It was a familiar tale, and Lex had seen the effects of greed like Schiller's more than once, and not just in Texas. But, like everything else in the state, greed seemed bigger than life here, seemed to flourish under the hot sun, like some sort of desert plant that needed little rain. Give it a place to set down roots, and in a week you'd need an ax to kill it. And if it was left alone, as Clay Schiller's greed had been, then it would take more than an ax to get rid of it. Greed like that was insatiable. It fed on blood and bone, chewed up men and property like a hungry scavenger.

Anna finally stopped, raised her eyes a little to see if he was looking at her, and when she realized he was, gave him a faint smile.

"Quite a story, Miss Kraus."

"I'm so ashamed. Ashamed of the way I spoke to you last night and ashamed that we stood by and let this happen. But I don't know what—"

"You don't have to explain anything to me, Anna. Neither does your father. I know how easily something like this can happen."

"It might be best for everyone if you let it go," she said. "If you make trouble, it will just be worse for all of us. There's been enough killing."

"I can't just walk away from this, Anna."

"What are you going to do?"

"The first thing I want to do is have a little talk with Mr. Schiller. After that, who knows...?"

"He'll kill you."

"I don't think so. I'll send word to Austin and get some help down here as soon as I can. It might take a few days, but the Rangers aren't going to be intimidated by the likes of Clayton Schiller."

"They can't stay here forever."

"Neither can Schiller. Just let me handle it, Anna. It'll be all right. I promise."

He stood up. She reached out a hand and closed her long fingers around his wrist. "Please, be careful."

"I didn't get to be this old without being careful, Miss Kraus." He laughed, trying to reassure her, but she had only a thin smile in response.

Lex walked to the door and turned as he stepped through. Anna was still sitting in the chair. Her shoulders shook, but she made no sound. Lex closed the door softly.

Out in the street for the first time in several days, he felt as if he'd been locked in a cave for months. The morning sunlight was harsh, and he knew the heat would be merciless well before noon. The first thing he wanted to do was to send a wire to Austin, to tell Major Podell what was happening and to ask for help. At first, he had been surprised that his initial wire had drawn no response, but now he was beginning to wonder if it had been sent at all.

He spotted the sign, its paint faded and peeling, and crossed the street to climb onto the boardwalk. The telegraph office sat between a pair of saloons. One, the Tinhorn, was boarded up; the other, called the Edelweiss, was already open for business, despite the early hour. It belonged to Schiller, according to Anna, although it was a recent acquisition. The boards on the other barroom were still new. As he walked past, he could smell the fresh wood. Its proprietor had left hurriedly, not two days after Schiller bought out the owner of the Edelweiss, at a bargain price. No good-byes, no forwarding address. There one day and gone the next. The pattern was a familiar one.

Lex stopped in front of the telegraph office and turned to take in the town. Laidlaw was dusty, a little shabby around its edges, and the curtained windows of the second-story rooms seemed dispirited somehow. Even the fresh paint, which glistened faintly under a coating of beige dust on a few of the buildings, couldn't change the first impression, that Laidlaw was a place on the edge of catastrophe.

Stepping through the open door into the telegraph office, Lex found himself the object of wide-eyed scrutiny. A scrawny kid, who might have weighed a hundred and twenty with a sack of flour on his shoulder, gawked at Lex.

"You the agent?" Lex asked.

The kid didn't respond right away. Lex had to repeat his question before the kid blinked. He rubbed his prominent Adam's apple with the back of one bony hand. Then he nodded.

"The name's Cranshaw."

The kid made no response except for a sudden swallow, which bobbed the prominent bulge on his slender neck.

"I want to send a telegram. I want to check on another wire, too. Should be a response by now."

"What wire?"

"The sheriff sent it for me a couple of days ago, to Austin. To Major Earl Podell. The reply would be addressed to me."

"No, sir. He never done that."

"Sure he did. I asked Sheriff Cannon to do it, and he said he would."

"No, sir. He never did."

"You the only agent?"

The kid nodded. "Yes, sir, I am." There was a hint of pride in the response, although Lex couldn't imagine why.

"All right, then. Let me send another one."

"Who to?"

"Major Podell."

The kid looked over his shoulder for a second, as if checking with some unseen supervisor, then shrugged.

He shoved a pad aross his desk. "Write 'er out," he said.

Lex printed his message, crossed out a few words, then rewrote it. When he was satisfied, he slid the pad back across the desk. The kid counted the words, then looked up. "Four bits," he said.

Lex fished a coin out of his pocket, flipped it to the kid, then waited while the clerk started to tap out his message. He sent it twice, then waited for the receipt acknowledgment. But nothing happened.

"That's funny," the boy said.

"Problem?"

"No response. Line must be down. Shouldn't be, though. The Comanche used to take them out all the time, but there hasn't been any trouble like that for a couple of years."

"Send it again later, would you?" Lex asked.

When the kid nodded, once more looking over his shoulder for a split second, Lex said. "I'll stop back in a half hour. Should be an answer as soon as you get through."

The clerk snapped a salute that was about as ragged as Laidlaw itself, and Lex went back outside. Already he could feel the temperature rising. He moved along the walk and stepped into the Edelweiss. Half a dozen men lined the bar, most of them cowhands, muttering among themselves. One man, his suit rumpled, and the tail of a shirt sticking out under his jacket, stood by himself at the far end of the bar.

Lex crossed the barroom, checking the silent faces

that turned to him one by one, then turned back to their drinks and conversation. He ordered a bourbon, waited while the barkeep poured the whiskey, then took a sip. The barman stood across the bar from him, swiping at the wood with a damp cloth. "A dollar," he said.

"Kind of steep, isn't it?" Lex grinned, but the barkeep never changed his surly expression.

"That's the going rate. You find another bar, you can drink there, cowboy."

Lex paid, took another sip of the cheap, weak whiskey, and set the glass on the bar. It burned a little going down, but he'd had worse. After ordering another, he paid, then moved to a table. The cowhands, he was almost certain, would be some of Schiller's men.

They ignored him, and when he had nursed the second drink as long as he could, he downed the last few drops, got up, walked over to the bar to leave the glass, then went outside.

He noticed that the door of the telegraph office was now closed. He peered inside and turned the knob. The door opened easily, and the clerk, napping at his desk, didn't look up.

"You get through?" Lex asked.

The kid didn't answer him. Lex knit his brows, puzzled by the silence. He'd expected the kid to bolt upright and make some lame excuse about how he wasn't really sleeping, just thinking. But the kid hadn't moved.

Then he saw the stain on the pad and, beyond it, a small puddle all the way back to the edge of the desk on either side of the motionless clerk. He reached over the desk and shook the kid by the shoulder. The clerk's head flopped to one side.

He wasn't sleeping. His throat had been cut.

EX backed out of the office, closing the door again. He had spotted the sheriff's office earlier, and he headed straight toward it. A deputy was on duty. When Lex asked for the sheriff, the deputy scowled and told him Cannon would be in in about an hour.

"Get him now," Lex snapped. He leaned across the desk, conscious of the twitching muscle along the edge of his jaw.

For a moment the deputy seemed off balance. He stared at Lex as if wondering how to handle him. "Who the hell are you that I should give a good goddamn what you want?"

Lex leaned all the way across the desk and grabbed a fistful of the deputy's shirt. "Just get him." He twisted the cloth until he heard the first sharp hint of tearing, then shook the bigger man back and forth for a few seconds until the deputy clasped both of his hands over Lex's fist.

Lex let go then, and when the deputy's eyes had stopped bugging out of his head, he shrugged, tugged his shirt back into some semblance of order, took a deep breath, and asked, "You want to tell me why? Sheriff Cannon's gonna want to know why I drug him out of bed."

Lex was on the edge of losing his patience. "Murder good enough for you?"

"Depends," the deputy sneered, "on who got kilt." He was a big man, his face sunburned, his mustache bleached and drooping down over thin lips. He had big hands with prominent knuckles, and they sat curled on the desk in front of him like a pair of mutant armadillos.

"The telegraph clerk," Lex told him. "Young kid maybe twenty, twenty-one. Skinny as a bird's leg."

"Davey Wilkins? You're kidding. Who in hell'd want to kill him? Don't weigh but as much as a handful of oats. No need to kill a boy like that." The news seemed somehow to have civilized the deputy, as if the realization of the clerk's mortality had made him suddenly conscious of his own, and of how dangerously close to it he had come by baiting the man in front of him.

"Somebody had a need," Lex said, "because he sure as hell is dead. Somebody cut his throat."

"Naw." The deputy seemed to wilt then like a lettuce

leaf left in the sun. He shook his head like a man trying to get water out of his ear.

"Go check," Lex told him. "The body's in the telegraph office. And whoever did it can't be far away, because I had Wilkins send a wire not twenty minutes before I found his body, and he was alive and kicking."

"Let's go see," the deputy said. "What'd you say your name was?"

"I didn't. It's Cranshaw. Lex Cranshaw."

The deputy leaned back in his chair, narrowed his eyes a bit, and stared at Lex. "You're that Ranger rode in half dead a few days ago with Gunther Kleinhalder's body in tow, ain't you?"

Lex nodded.

"Folks seem to have a way of dying around you, don't they?" the deputy asked. He seemed sorry as soon as he closed his mouth, but Lex ignored the implication.

"This doesn't seem to be a very safe town. You ask me, maybe the sheriff ought to be doing something about that. It's his job, isn't it?"

"You want to tell Sheriff Cannon that your own self, you be my guest. I sure as hell won't tell him." The deputy got up from his chair and stepped around the battered desk with exaggerated care. He led the way out of the office, clapping a hat on his pale hair and squinting up at the sky as he stepped into the street.

Lex kept up with the bigger man's long strides, his

head feeling a little light, but otherwise unaffected by the sudden exertion. He was starting to feel more in control of himself, as if his body once again knew who was in charge.

When they reached the telegraph office, the deputy stopped for a long moment. He turned to look at Lex, resting his hand on the knob, then pushing the door open and leaning forward to peer into the darkness.

"He's at the desk," Lex said, placing a hand on the deputy's back and giving him a little impetus into the shadowy interior.

The big man moved cautiously, edged around the desk, and took a quick look. "That's Davey Wilkins, all right. And he's deader'n a doornail. You better wait here while I get Sheriff Cannon."

"I'm not going anyplace," Lex said, moving aside to let the deputy back through the door. "Make it quick, would you?"

The deputy nodded, all the starch gone out of him now. He hotfooted it up the block while Lex stood in the doorway, leaning against the frame and watching him. The deputy unhitched his horse from the rail in front of the sheriff's office, swung up into the saddle, then dug his spurs in and clucked to his chestnut stallion. The horse kicked up tiny clouds of dust that seemed to hang in the air almost motionless for several seconds, then collapsed and disappeared.

While he waited for the sheriff, Lex tried to piece together what he knew. It wasn't much. Clay Schiller seemed to hover over Laidlaw like a black cloud. But for the moment there was no obvious reason to suspect Schiller had anything to do with Davey Wilkins's death. Still, there were no other candidates. Cannon, who was securely nestled in Schiller's pocket, according to Anna Kraus, had not sent a telegram, as Lex had asked. That made Cannon look bad, but it didn't prove anything. And yet it seemed certain that someone was very concerned that Lex not be in touch with the outside, concerned enough to kill a harmless kid to make sure the message didn't get out.

That seemed to point to Schiller again, but it was a tenuous link. It wasn't likely that Cannon would volunteer any suggestions, at least not useful ones, but Lex would just have to wait and see.

It took Cannon twenty minutes. He was riding hell for leather when he broke over a ridge at the north end of town, and he didn't slow until he was within thirty yards of the telegraph office. He slid out of the saddle like a man who had been born to ride, and he stomped onto the boardwalk, his suspenders still draped over his hips.

"What the hell happened here, Cranshaw?"

Lex shook his head. "Your guess is as good as mine, Sheriff. I saw Wilkins this morning, gave him a message to send. He couldn't get through, and when I came back twenty minutes later he was dead."

"You see anybody near the office?" Cannon fished a tobacco pouch out of his shirt pocket, painstakingly rolled a thick cigarette, and replaced the pouch. He looked at Lex then, his mouth open expectantly.

"Nope. But then, I wasn't really looking. No reason to expect something like this."

Cannon took a deep breath. He knelt beside the desk, took a look at the body, and turned away. "Jesus Christ! Poor Davey..." Stabbing the cigarette into his mouth, he took a match from his back pocket, struck it on the side of the desk, and sucked on the cigarette until he was sure it would stay lit. Then he flicked the match out with a thumbnail and flipped it through the open door.

"Seems like somebody besides you doesn't want me to get in touch with Austin," Lex said.

Still on his knees alongside the desk, Cannon snapped his head around and glared at Lex. "What do you mean, besides me? What's that supposed to mean?"

"You didn't send the wire I asked you to send." Lex spoke quietly, trying to avoid a flat-out accusation.

Cannon's face changed then. He nodded. "You're right. I'm sorry for that. I forgot all about it. But I don't see any connection."

"I do."

"You want to explain that?"

"Shouldn't be necessary."

"I'm telling you it is." Cannon sucked on the cigarette, jerked it away from his lips, glared at it for a moment, then stuck it back into his mouth.

Lex shrugged. "You don't send a message. I try to do it myself, but somebody kills the clerk. What would you think if you were in my place?"

"It don't look innocent, I'll grant you that, Cranshaw. But I still don't see why it should matter to anybody whether you send a wire or not." He took one more drag on the cigarette, then dropped it to the floor and ground it out with the toe of one boot.

"Not even Clayton Schiller?"

Cannon stood up. "You accusing Mr. Schiller of killing Wilkins?"

"No, just asking a question. You think he might have reason to want to keep me from getting in touch with the capital? Or am I just imagining things?"

"I don't see why he would give a damn who you're in touch with."

"Then you aren't looking too hard. The way I hear it, Schiller's been riding roughshod over half the county. A company of Rangers just might interfere with that habit. That seems like all the reason he'd need."

"Listen. You want to be careful before you go accusing a man like Mr. Schiller of something like that. Especially without cause."

"What might happen? Maybe I'd end up like Wilkins, is that it?"

"I didn't say that."

"But that's what you meant, isn't it? You're his man, I understand that. But maybe you ought to give some thought to just how deep in his pocket you want to be."

Cannon took a step toward Lex, his hand dropping to the butt of his Colt. But Lex shook his head. "You don't want to do that, Sheriff. Believe me, you really don't."

"Cranshaw, I'm gonna forget what you just said. But I'm warning you, you talk like that around town, I won't be responsible for what might happen."

"And just what might that be, Sheriff?"

"Mr. Schiller has a bad temper. And some of his hands ain't much more civilized than a pack of wolves. But you know how that is, Cranshaw. Things get rough kind of easy out here. It don't take much to light the powder."

"Seems like somebody ought to change that."

"Not you, Cranshaw."

"We'll have to see about that."

"I think you ought to let me handle this. In fact, I think it would be best for everybody concerned if you were to ride on out of here before anybody else gets hurt."

"Seems to me like people get hurt all the time around here, whether I'm around or not. Kleinhalder, Schliemann, Rafferty, McQuade, Ross, Wilkins... Just how long is the list, anyway, Sheriff?"

"I'll handle it, Cranshaw, dammit. I'm telling you, now. Just stay out of it!"

"I'm staying right here, Sheriff. But you got a job to do, and if you don't do it, then I'm here to tell you it'll damn sure get done anyhow."

"Cranshaw, you get in my way and I guarantee you'll be one sorry feller. I don't give a damn whether you're a Ranger or not. People don't come around here and tell me how to do my job."

"Maybe they should, Sheriff," Lex said. "Maybe they should."

10

LEX walked to the livery stable to get his horse. The big bay had been put up by Doc Kraus, a week paid in advance. When the liveryman brought him out, Lex checked the cinch, then pulled his Winchester carbine from the boot. After checking with the stableman to make sure it was all right, he went into a small office tucked in the front corner of the stable, dropped his saddlebags on the floor, and sat down to clean the rifle. He reloaded the magazine, then poured a handful of shells into his pocket, tucked the ammunition box and cleaning kit back into the bags, and walked back to the horse, which was standing off to one side and muttering in anticipation.

Clayton Schiller's ranch, the Flying S, was ten miles north of town. Lex wanted to get a feel for the countryside and planned on a leisurely ride that would take him over a snaking route past several of the small ranches that had been abandoned under Schiller's relentless pressure. Lex thought it would be useful to see what it was Schiller wanted, as if what the rancher coveted might suggest some way he could be stopped.

According to Anna, a number of small property owners still held out, but their number was shrinking. Kleinhalder was the latest victim, but he would not be the last, she was certain. The sun was well up in the sky by the time Laidlaw fell away behind Lex. Twice he had felt a warning tingle along the back of his neck and had looked over his shoulder, half expecting to see a trio of gunmen—flat, featureless paper cutouts, as anonymous as the three men who had gunned Kleinhalder down. But both times he found himself staring back into the empty, sun-baked plains.

Ahead, the low silhouette of a small ranch house broke the horizon. Situated just below the crest of small hill, it appeared to be deserted, but Lex thought it worth a look. He clucked to the bay, sawed the reins enough to get the horse to change direction, then squeezed the bay between his knees, causing the big horse to spurt ahead.

As he drew closer, he could see that the place was uninhabited. The windows were all broken, and the burned-out shell of a barn, all but overgrown by weeds, stood off to the left. A mound of split rails, themselves bleached bone gray by the sun, had been crudely stacked behind the ruined barn.

Lex dismounted and walked the last fifty yards. Letting the reins trail on the ground, he moved into the weeds. His boots crunched on charred hunks of wood half hidden by the growth. Something clinked dully, and he dropped to one knee and pushed weeds aside to find the twisted remains of a plow, the blade melted into an amorphous lump of metal.

Straightening, he peered through the grass, spotted another hump ten feet away, and walked toward it. After using the toe of one boot to push the grass aside, he found himself staring into the vacant sockets of the flame-blackened skull of a cow. The rib cage was shrunken and charred, looking for all the world like the ruins of a tiny ship put to the torch.

He wondered why the house hadn't been torched and moved toward it, approaching the rear, where two vacant windows gaped blindly toward the northwest. Leaning through the shattered frame of the nearer window, he surveyed the wreckage inside. The furniture—a table top still plainly showing the bite of an ax; several chairs, their seats splintered; an old upright piano, its back laid open and its strings sprung loose, severed in the middle, and coiled like the hair of a manic Medusa—showed that the inhabitants had not left by choice.

Climbing in through the broken window, he stepped on the shards of the family china, piled in a heap against the wall. Moving into another room, this one full of rumpled bedclothes and the remains of a mattress heaped on a shattered bed frame, he shook his head. The last room, a small one, obviously that of a child, was as ravaged as the others.

An armless doll, its head lolling at an unnatural angle, lay on the floor. Lex took a deep breath, backed out of the room, and walked through the front door, which hung from a single hinge. Standing out in the sun, he knew why the house had not been torched. This way it was more effective testimony to what it meant to defy Clayton Schiller. If it had been burned to the ground, in six months the weeds would have covered it all, as they had covered the barn, leaving little more than another thickening green mound. Now, with the door yawning in a mute scream, the empty windows gaping like blind eyes, people would know, people would remember.

Lex walked back to the bay. The horse, oblivious to the ruins and their meaning, chomped idly at bunch grass over near the stack of rails. Lex grabbed the reins and climbed back into the saddle. He pushed the horse north, up over the hill and down the far side, leaving the monument to Schiller's greed behind.

Ahead, a thin coil of smoke reared up like a cobra, and Lex headed for it, curious to know what lay at its base. It took a quarter hour to get close enough. And the smoke had thickened into a broad ribbon of dark gray.

He was still a mile away from the fire when he heard the first gunshot. The sharp crack was followed by a volley, and Lex spurred the bay. He dropped down a steep hill and lost sight of the column of smoke for a few seconds; then, as he started up the next rise, it gradually reappeared.

Sporadic gunfire continued to shatter the silence. He was close enough now to hear someone shouting. Lex topped the next rise and for the first time was able to see where the smoke was coming from. A barn, its roof ablaze, one wall a sheet of flame, sent a shower of sparks up on the heated air, like pale stars against the near-black smoke.

A small house, its sides sparkling with a fresh coat of paint, stood off to his left. At the bottom of a broad valley a shallow stream snaked through the grass, its surface catching the sun on its ripples and scattering blades of white light in every direction.

Several men lay on the ground, arrayed in a broad arc around the front of the small house. Alongside the burning barn, several horses reared up, terrified by the flames and kicking at the rails of a corral.

Lex drew the Winchester instinctively. He clicked off the safety and levered a shell home. The house was under siege, but he didn't know why. He was tempted to charge in, gun blazing, and pin the siege force down from behind, but he couldn't afford to make a mistake.

Angling toward a small stand of cottonwoods to the left of the barn, Lex galloped across the creek and circled in behind the barn. The voices were distinct now. Someone in the house was shouting at the men. "You tell Clay Schiller he ain't gonna run me off, Pardee."

The only answer was another volley from the prostrate cowboys. Bullets chipped at the house, and a pane of glass shattered. One bullet passed through a front window and shattered glass on its way out a rear window. Lex dismounted and ducked into a crouch. The exertion made his shoulder ache, but he couldn't afford to worry about it.

Racing toward the rear of the house, he spotted a man coming in from the far side, a torch in his hand. Lex dropped to one knee and fired a warning shot. The bullet whistled close to the torchbearer, he dropped to the ground, his head swiveling back and front while he tried to locate the source of the bullet.

Lex hugged the ground, and the man with the torch, getting to his feet again, resumed his charge toward the house. This time Lex took careful aim. He fired again; the bullet caught the man in the thigh, and he went down. The torch flew from his grasp and landed in some tall grass, brittle and dried by the sun. The grass caught almost immediately, and the first puffs of white smoke soon turned a dirty gray as the flames spread out from the torch.

The man got up and started to hop, trying to keep his weight off the wounded leg. He fell again and this time wasn't able to get up. The flames raced toward him, but Lex was more concerned with the house. The grass came close before ending in a patch of tilled earth staked for some sort of vegetable garden.

Lex raced toward the rear of the house, conscious that the defender might take him for one of Schiller's men. He zigzagged, reached the rear wall of the house, and waited for the flames to reach the garden. A single tongue of fire licked at the small white pickets setting the garden off, then died.

He heard a scream then and looked back to where the wounded man was beating at his clothes as the grass fire surrounded him like a swarm of hornets. A single piercing shriek, its pitch climbing to an inhuman howl, ended abruptly. Lex moved toward the nearer of two rear windows.

The glass was shattered, and Lex shouted, "You all right in there?"

A bullet ripped at the window frame, and Lex ducked back out of the line of fire.

"I'm a friend," Lex shouted.

"Liar. I got no friends around here." Another shot cracked, tearing another hunk out of the window frame.

Lex shouted a second time. "Hold your fire. I'm coming in."

"You do and you're a dead man."

Lex tossed his Winchester inside, heard it land on the floor and clatter to a halt. This was one of those times when he wished the Rangers were like other peace officers. A badge would have made this a whole lot safer and whole lot easier. But Rangers didn't carry badges. You were what you were, and that was all there was to it. If you needed a piece of tin to do your job, then you weren't cut out for it.

Lex eased in front of the window, his empty hands held palms forward, then ducked through the window, waiting for the bullet that would put an end to him. But it never came. He was inside and found himself staring at a round man in soiled overalls, who was lying on the floor and staring back at the crazy man who'd just come through his window.

"Who in hell are you?" the man asked.

"Name's Cranshaw. Texas Rangers, Company F."

"What do you want?"

Before Lex could answer, another volley crackled from the front of the house, two bullets ripping through the last unbroken pane of glass in the front window and slamming into the wall behind him. He dropped to the floor and crawled toward the farmer.

"What do you want?" the man asked a second time.

"I want to help you."

"Why?"

"Why not?"

The farmer shrugged. "Hell, it ain't like I don't need it. I thank you, I guess."

"Who are those men?"

"Some of Clay Schiller's hired goons, I expect. None of 'em been close enough for me to tell for sure. But he's been leaning on me, just like he leaned on other folks. I told him to stick it in his hat, but he's a hard man to buck."

"You aim to buck him?"

"Hell, Mr. Cranshaw, I got no choice."

Just then Lex heard a whimper, but it was choked off almost as soon as it registered.

The farmer noticed and said, "That'd be baby Jesse. He ain't but a few months old, and Mavis's tryin' to keep him quiet."

"You mean to tell me there's a woman and child in

here, and those men are—"

"Hell, I got three, but the older ones know not to cry. This ain't the first time we had trouble like this. Comanche and Kiowa come through here few years back. This ain't nothing compared to that. 'Course, I'm a lot older now." Then, sticking out a hand, the farmer said, "Name's James Kensington."

"Pleased to meet you, Mr. Kensington."

"Bet you wish the circumstances was better, though, don't you?" He laughed then, easily and with a full-throated rumble that shook his stocky frame.

"Sure do."

Lex moved over to grab his Winchester and then scooted over next to one of the windows. "There's five of them, that I saw, plus the one around back."

"Around back?" Kensington seemed startled.

"Not a problem now. He was going to torch the house, but I got to him first."

"Bastards already burned the damn barn." Kensington popped up and fired twice, then dropped below the window again.

A moment later one of Schiller's hands got to his feet and darted forward. Lex dropped him with a clean shot, and the man fell on his belly, his legs twitching for several seconds before he lay still.

Another man eased forward, barely visible over the grass as he tried to get to the wounded man. Kensington spotted him, wet his trigger finger on his lips, and took aim. He squeezed off an easy shot. The crawling man popped up for an instant, his body arced like a hooked trout, then disappeared.

"Bastards!" Kensington shouted.

For the next fifteen minutes there was total silence. It was finally broken by the sound of hooves on the dusty hillside.

"They'll be back," Kensington said.

"Not if we get to Schiller first."

Kensington laughed. "You got big ideas, Mr. Cranshaw."

"It's a big country, Mr. Kensington. Seems like it ought to be big enough for you *and* Clayton Schiller."

"Tell him that."

"I aim to."

11

CLAYTON Schiller's ranch was more than impressive. The house was huge. A three-story building, it sat on top of a hill, surrounded by willows and cottonwoods thick enough to keep it shaded from the worst of the summer heat, but not so thick there wasn't a view of the valleys surrounding it on every side.

A wide, sluggish creek meandered lazily across the floor of the valley dead ahead. Stands of willows were bunched along the creekbank, their swooping limbs drooping almost to the ground, their freight of silvery leaves rustling in the hot late-morning sun.

The barn, the stables, and the bunkhouse were lower down and in excellent repair, suggesting that Clayton Schiller was doing very well for himself. Lex rode through the gate, passing under an ornately carved arch that spelled out Schiller's name and was crowned with a relief of the Flying S brand. It reminded Lex of royal crests he'd seen in books about England and France. He glanced up at the arch as he passed under it.

He wasn't twenty yards inside the fence when three cowhands came galloping toward him from a stand of willows off to the left. As they rode closer, the hands drew their guns, slowing their mounts to a walk. The apparent leader, a small man with the lean face of a greyhound, its skin a dark bronze, held up a hand. His two companions reined in, and the small man walked his mount, a small pinto, probably an Indian pony, to a point on the dusty lane about twenty yards ahead of Lex, then turned his horse sideways.

The small man's left side was toward Lex, the gun in his left hand pointed vaguely in Lex's direction, not dead on, but close enough to seem more than a little unfriendly.

"You lost, partner?" The man steadied his horse, reaching out to pat it on the shoulder, but he never took his eyes off Lex.

"This the Schiller ranch?"

The man nodded.

"Then no, I'm not lost."

"You got business with Mr. Schiller?"

"That depends on Mr. Schiller," Lex said.

"I asked you a question, cowboy. You want to answer me or not?"

Lex took a deep breath before responding. "I already

answered you. I said it depends on Mr. Schiller. Why don't you let him decide?"

"You mind telling me what it might be?"

"Are you Mr. Schiller?"

The man clucked once, sucked his teeth for a couple of seconds, then turned to look at his companions, still fifty feet away, still holding their sidearms, both pointed directly at Lex. "Man wants to know am I Mr. Schiller. You believe that?" He shook his head in disbelief.

The men laughed, the sudden, husky rattle making their mounts a little restless. Both horses pawed at the dry grass, the muffled thud of their hooves on the grassy turf like the beat of small drums covered with a comforter.

Then, turning back to Lex, the leader of the trio said, "No, I ain't Mr. Schiller. The fact that you don't even know that means you don't have no business with him."

Lex draped his hands over his saddle horn. "I think you ought to let him decide that."

"You do, do you?"

"Yes, sir, I surely do. Fact is, if you don't get out of my way, there might be trouble. I don't think Mr. Schiller would like that."

The man smiled, working on a chaw of tobacco, then ejected a stream of amber juice through a gap in his stained teeth. "Trouble, huh?"

Lex nodded. "That's right."

"You think you can give us trouble? Three to one.

Don't you even know how to count? Them's long odds, even for a tough customer like yourself."

The two hands eased their mounts a little closer.

Lex didn't answer. Something about the little man seemed familiar, but it was an elusive familiarity, slipping away like quicksilver through thick and clumsy fingers whenever he tried to pin it down.

The silence thickened, the snorting of the two subordinates' horses the only sound. Lex let the quiet grow longer. He watched the little man, alert to the slightest change in posture, the least tautening of muscle. But the man seemed quite relaxed, even a little amused. "You don't mind tellin' me what this is all about, do you?"

"Actually, I do."

The man smiled. "Look, partner. I'm the foreman around here. Mr. Schiller's an important man. I walk in to him and tell him somebody wants to see him about something, but I don't know what 'cause he won't tell me, what do you think Mr. Schiller will say?"

"I don't know the man. I don't know what he'd say. I know what he *should* say, though."

"And what's that?"

"Let's find out what he wants."

The little man laughed outright. Under the loud bellow, Lex heard the snick of a hammer cocking, and he yanked his Colt from its holster. "Don't!" he barked.

The little man turned to the two hands, one of whom had frozen in the act of aiming. "Put it up, dammit," he snapped. The hand glared at Lex, released the hammer, and lowered his gun, but he didn't put it in its holster.

"You got to excuse Roy," the little man said. "He's a little jumpy. Mr. Schiller's a powerful man in these parts. He's got enemies, and we got to make sure you ain't one."

"Not yet, I'm not," Lex said.

"What's that supposed to mean?"

"It means I don't know the man. It means I got no reason to think he's an enemy. Yet."

"And when you make up your mind...?"

"That depends, doesn't it?"

Once more the little man laughed. "I suppose it do." He chuckled. "I suppose it do. You got sand, partner, I'll give you that." Cocking his head to one side, he studied Lex for a long moment before asking, "You mind telling me what your name is?"

"Cranshaw. Lex Cranshaw."

"Don't think I've ever seen you before. You new around here?"

"Passing through."

The little man nodded. "Passing through," he echoed. "You looking for work? 'Cause if you are, we're full up."

"Nope. I got work."

"What kind?"

"Texas Ranger."

The little man tilted his head back. "Uh-huh. You're the one... the one Sheriff Cannon told us about. You brung in that dead sodbuster, ain't that right?"

"If you mean Gunther Kleinhalder, that's right. The way I hear it, though, he was just a hardworking man trying to make a living."

"On somebody else's land, he was. You here to look into that?"

"Yes."

"Well, I suppose there's no harm in it." Turning to the two hands, he said, "Roy, you and Rance stay here. Keep an eye peeled." He turned back to Lex then. "Follow me," he said.

The ride to the house took almost ten minutes. The little man seemed to be in no hurry. He kept glancing back over his shoulder as if to make certain that Lex was following him, but he made no conversation. As they started up the long, winding approach to the main house, the building looked even more imposing. Lex remembered fairy tales from his childhood, stories of fabulous castles floating on clouds, where everything was gold and silver and the women wore silk and diamonds big as eggs. Schiller's house seemed to hang over him in the air like that, almost floating on the sere green of the grassy hillside.

He had to keep telling himself not to be impressed, to pay attention to the man instead of what he owned, but it wasn't going to be easy.

They reached level ground at the front of the house and dismounted in the shade of several tall cottonwoods. Both men tied off, and the little man led the way up the stairs onto a broad front porch. Tall glass doors, open to admit the hilltop breeze, led into a high-ceilinged foyer, its polished parquet floor gleaming with recent oiling.

The little foreman walked down a corridor and turned once more to make certain he still had his unwelcome guest in tow, then disappeared through a doorway on the left. Lex stepped in to see a tall, thin man getting up from behind a mahogany desk and slipping into an expensive eastern-style suit jacket. When the jacket was in place, he studied Lex for a long moment, his blue eyes restless, his close-cropped white hair and mustache elegant and perfectly in place.

Stepping out from behind the desk, he positioned himself in front of it, then leaned back against the front edge, bracing himself with a hand beside either hip. His gleaming boots squeaked as the new leather tried to accommodate itself to the movement.

"What the hell you bothering me for, Cranshaw?" he asked.

"I'm the man who—"

"I know who you are. Answer my damn question."

"Gunther Kleinhalder was killed in cold blood. Some people think maybe you—"

"I don't give a damn what people think. Besides, it's not your affair. It's the sheriff's business. Whoever did it, Pete Cannon will find them."

"If he looks."

"That's his job."

"What I hear is that you tell him what his job is. You tell him to look for the killers, did you?"

"You snotty son of a bitch! Are you accusing me?

Because if you are, I'll let my attorney tell you how things are."

"I know how things are, Mr. Schiller. I know a few people are dead, people who were tending their own lives, minding their own business. People who shouldn't be dead."

"I can't help that. This is rough country. People who can't take care of themselves shouldn't try to live here." He paused, his eyes motionless for the first time since Lex had entered the study. They seemed to bore into Lex, looking for something, like a geologist taking core samples. Schiller was trying to decide exactly what this impertinent man was made of, how he dared to confront him.

Lex broke the silence. "Can you take care of yourself, Mr. Schiller?"

"Damn right I can."

"That's what I'm here for," the little man said.

Lex looked hard at the foreman. "You think so, do you?"

"You can put that in the bank, Cranshaw."

Lex shook his head. "Not Mr. Schiller's bank, I won't. I wouldn't dare."

"Get out of here," Schiller snapped. "You come around here again, I'll have you shot."

"I wouldn't recommend that, Mr. Schiller."

"I don't give a damn what you'd recommend."

"You will."

12

LEX stopped on the first rise. He turned to look back at the massive home of Clayton Schiller. The white mansion no longer looked so imposing. Having met the man who built it, who lived in it, had somehow diminished it, as if the house partook in some way of Schiller's own limitations.

There was no longer room to doubt that Schiller was up to something. For an ordinary man, it was still a long way from arrogance and intolerance to murder, but maybe not for a man like Schiller. The Clayton Schillers of the world recognized no limits on themselves, only those on others. To wish something was to want to see it happen; to covet something was to own it. And it seemed clear that Clayton Schiller was a man with big ideas, both about himself and about his role in Laidlaw County.

Catching him in the act was out of the question. Clayton Schiller wouldn't be caught dead with a smoking Colt in his fist. That sort of thing was beneath him. He preferred to have such chores done for him. What, after all, was money for? What good was influence if you couldn't wield it with all the subtlety of a broadax to get your way?

No, there would be no blood on those impeccably manicured hands. Which left only one alternative: Lex would have to get his hands on someone who worked for Schiller, someone who knew what had been done for the would-be baron, someone who was willing to talk about it, willing to turn the key on the cell door after Lex put Schiller behind bars. That meant finding a man with a conscience, someone who had worked for Schiller, or still did, but who was disgusted both with his employer and with himself, disgusted enough to admit his own mistakes in order to make a clean breast of it.

It might be easier to find El Dorado. Lex Cranshaw knew that, but he was not easily deterred. He would stick to Schiller like a burr to a pony's tail, hang on no matter which way he was pushed or pulled, twisted or turned, and if there was a God in heaven—something about which Lex was far from certain—and if that God was as sickened by the likes of Clayton Schiller as Lex himself—which was equally debatable—then there was a chance. It was a slim one, but it was better than nothing. And besides, he told himself, it's all I've got.

And somehow Heinrich Kraus and his daughter

seemed like the logical place to start. The doctor obviously knew more than he was willing to say. But he seemed to be on the verge of a change of heart, as if whatever he knew bothered him more than a little, bothered him enough, maybe, that a push in the right direction, at the right time, might just be enough to topple him off the fence. And Anna, too, seemed to be troubled by what she knew, troubled in some way that had nothing to do with the murder of Karl Schliemann. But she was hard to read, harder even than her father who was by no means an open book.

Lex took one last lingering look at the house on the hill, wheeled his bay, and started down the far side of the slope. He didn't look back again until he was certain he was far enough below the ridgeline that he would not be able to see the house.

Confronting Schiller had been risky, maybe even foolhardy. He knew that. If Schiller was not above murder, then the removal of one pesky Ranger, no more than a chinch bug to a man like Schiller, would be about as significant as crushing a flea under a thumbnail. On the other hand, someone had already tried to kill him, someone to whom Lex represented a threat. Other than Clayton Schiller, there was a decided absence of viable candidates.

From here on out he would have to take more than his usual care. There was the chance, however slight, that the men who had tried to kill him were acting on their own. But now that Schiller knew about him, the threat could only be greater.

At the top of every rise, Lex paused long enough to make certain he wasn't being followed. It seemed almost too soon for Schiller to make a move, if he was planning on it, but Lex knew he would be in danger every minute that Schiller was allowed to trample over the people of Laidlaw and Laidlaw County. And unless he got suddenly lucky, he was on his own.

It occurred to him that he could try to send a wire on his own, but that seemed like a long shot. A man who would kill a harmless clerk would think nothing of sabotaging the telegraph lines. They hadn't been working when Davey Wilkins was killed, and Lex was willing to bet they still weren't working. Sooner or later, though, a repair crew would be sent out to find the break in the line. That might take three days or ten, but a man looking to protect himself would assume he didn't have much time. To Lex that meant another attempt to kill him would come sooner rather than later.

And he had one other possible source of information. A man with something on his conscience was likely to be looking to bury that troubling thought—or drown it. There was only one saloon in Laidlaw, so if he wanted to drink, such a man would have no choice. The saloon belonged to Schiller, but a man anxious to numb his conscience wouldn't be particular about who pocketed the price of the drinks, so long as they dulled his mind, let him forget his troubles, killed the painful ache in the back of his skull.

When he reached the outskirts of Laidlaw, it was early afternoon. Lex wanted to talk to Heinrich Kraus, but that could wait. He headed for the Edelweiss. Nearly a dozen horses were tied at the hitching rails in front of the saloon. The piano was clanking away, a Stephen Foster tune being sliced into unrecognizable pieces on the taut but desperately out-of-tune strings.

Lex walked in, took an empty table in the corner, and waited for a barmaid to approach him with a rustle of taffeta, her waist cinched into an hourglass by a corset that must have been painful and that played tricks with her voice, making it sound as if it were being squeezed out of her by a whalebone vise.

He ordered a beer, turned to watch the piano player adjust his sleeves, snap the garters back into place on the striped shirt, and begin his sledgehammer assault on another Foster melody, the tune this time barely different from the preceding rendition.

The barmaid came back with his beer. He paid, making sure there would be enough change for a tip, and took a long pull on the beer while he scanned the other patrons, watching them over the top of the mug as he sipped. He didn't want to be obvious, but he knew that he was playing a long shot, and he couldn't afford to miss the slightest clue. Once word got around, even a man with the tattered remnants of a conscience would realize it would be unwise to be seen talking to him.

Most of the drinkers were cowhands. They sat at tables in twos and threes, except for four men at the bar who seemed to be arguing good-naturedly about something, each in turn trying with little success to enlist the sympathies of the bartender. Most barkeeps knew that neutrality was the surest way to keep the customers happy. Take sides and you made as many enemies as friends.

Only one man stayed by himself, like Lex, at a corner table. The man, who looked to be in his middle twenties, was the same even bronze color as the rest of the hands. His dark brown hair, curly enough to suggest the possibility of some Mexican blood, sported a handlebar mustache that showed signs of having been ignored. Thick wrists protruded from rolled-up shirtsleeves. He stared morosely at the beer in his half-full mug, its head dwindled to a thin sheet of foam. It looked almost as if the man was trying to count the bubbles before they all burst. His eyes never wavered from the inside of the mug, and Lex watched for nearly a minute before the lids slid down over the black eyes. When they lifted again, it was only slowly, as if the man was on the verge of sleep.

One of the men at a nearby table leaned toward the brooding cowhand, nearly rising out of his chair. "Carlos," he slurred, "we need another hand for some poker. What say?"

The dark-eyed man lifted his gaze for a second, shook his head, then went back to examining his drink. He seemed more interested in watching it than in swallowing it, as if drinking was something he did only with difficulty, which meant either that he was not used to drinking or that he was near his limit and knew it.

"Come on, Carlos," the cowboy bellowed. "Do you good to lose *un poco dinero.*"

Once more the dark-eyed man shook his head. "No, thanks," he said.

"Carlos, come on," one of the other hands pleaded. "Can't let me be the only one to make Wheeler rich."

Carlos shook his head once more, this time not even bothering to lift his eyes. He hoisted the mug, took a long sip of the warm beer, and slapped the glass back down uncertainly. He looked closely at the table, like a man who hadn't expected it to be there at all or who was surprised to find it so close to the mug.

Lex was beginning to wonder whether he had found his man. He watched Carlos closely, but the man seemed oblivious to everyone in the bar, even the hands taunting him to join their card game. Approaching him here, now, would be a mistake, Lex realized. If he wanted to find out whether Carlos had anything to offer, he would have to get him alone. Too many cowhands, most of whom probably worked for Schiller, or wished they did, were in a position to overhear any conversation. Even being seen with Lex might be an invitation to pressure, or worse.

Lex sipped his beer slowly, hoping Carlos would not fall asleep at the table, in which case he would probably be taken upstairs to one of the hotel rooms to sleep it off or packed onto his horse and taken back to Schiller's bunkhouse, if he was one of the Flying S crew.

The piano player was still hacking Foster to ribbons, making up in energy what he lacked in technique. The jangling piano made it hard to hear conversation that wasn't shouted. Watching the cowhands, Lex eliminated them one by one, always coming back to Carlos as the most likely place to start. Carlos got up then, moving slowly, and went toward the back of the saloon. He went through a doorway to the left of the bar. At first, Lex thought he ought to follow, then realized the cowboy was probably just going to use the outhouse behind the saloon. The horses hitched out front probably included Carlos's mount.

Carlos reappeared, buttoning his pants. He seemed unaware that there was anyone else in the saloon. He moved back toward his table with the exaggerated slowness of a man who knows he is not quite in control of himself and wants to appear sober. He flopped down in his chair, and the barmaid spotted his raised hand. Without even checking with him, she had the bartender draw another beer. As she started toward him with the fresh drink, Carlos downed the last of his current drink, now almost flat, and pushed the empty mug across the table with the edge of a half-dollar fished from his pocket, then let the coin clatter onto the table, where it spun drunkenly for a couple of seconds before sputtering to a halt.

The butterfly doors swung inward, and Lex glanced up to see the little man from Schiller's ranch push through, followed by Roy and Rance, the third man from the crew at the gate. The little man looked around the bar, spotted Carlos, and came toward him, a scowl on his face.

"Carlos," he said, loud enough for everyone in the saloon to hear him, "where the hell you been, amigo?"

"Not your amigo," Carlos said, his words slurred a bit as he tried to make himself heard over the rattling piano.

The little man spotted Lex and changed course. He planted himself in front of Lex's table. "Cranshaw, you know who owns this place?" he demanded.

Lex nodded. "I can guess."

"Don't guess. Drink up and get out. Mr. Schiller don't want your money."

"You ask him about that?"

"Don't have to."

"Seems to me a man like Mr. Schiller probably wants all the money there is. Shouldn't make any difference to him where it comes from."

"It makes a difference," the little man said.

Lex smiled benignly and made no move to get up.

"You hear what I said?"

The piano had stopped now. Lex was aware of the utter silence. He knew, without looking, that all eyes were on him. The little man moved around the table, and Lex watched him, turning his head to keep the small man in the center of his field of vision. He knew the point of the maneuver was to get Roy and the other cowhand, Rance, out of his sight, but there was nothing he could do about that. The little man was the real threat.

"You gonna leave now, or you want to be helped out?"

Lex stood up, pushing the chair away from the backs of his legs with one heel. "Think I'll stay and have another beer," he said.

"The hell you will."

Lex saw the man's fingers curling and uncurling, edging toward the butt of his revolver. It was coming sooner than he had expected. With Cannon in Schiller's pocket, Lex was on his own in Laidlaw, and he knew it.

The sudden crack of a pistol, almost immediately followed by a groan, caused the little man to jerk his head away. Lex turned his eyes then and saw Roy grab his shoulder as a Colt clattered to the floor. Turning his head a little, Lex saw the smoking pistol in Carlos's hand.

"You don't have to backshoot nobody, amigo," Carlos said as Roy fell to one knee. "It ain't right."

The little man clenched his fist and took a step toward Carlos.

"I got five more, Mr. Pardee," Carlos said. He nodded as if to confirm the truth of the statement. "Five more, a-mi-go."

LEX watched Pardee and his underling drag the wounded Roy toward the door. The little man kept his eyes on Lex the whole time. At the butterfly doors, he stopped, letting Roy and Rance find their own way out. His face darkened a moment; then his eyes flicked toward Carlos. A second later he was gone, the doors clapping silently, their hinges creaking a little until they fell motionless.

Lex turned to Carlos, who was still sitting at his table, the pistol now resting on the scarred wood, his fingers curled loosely around the butt, his index finger hooked through the trigger guard.

Lex walked to the table and sat down. He waited for Carlos to acknowledge him, but the dark-haired cowhand never even looked at him. He just continued to stare into his beer as if fascinated by something he saw there.

"*Muchas gracias, amigo*," Lex said.

Carlos didn't move his head, but his eyes shifted slightly upward. Their expressionless gaze rested on Lex's face for a long, silent moment. Lex felt as if he were being sized up by a predator.

"I speak English," he said. Then, spitting one more word dipped in venom, he added, "Gringo."

Lex smiled. "No offense. I just thought maybe I could make things—"

"Look, I don't care what you thought. I ain't bothering you. Just leave me alone."

"What you did, that was a brave thing, Carlos. You saved my life."

"Yeah, well..." Rather than end the sentence, he shrugged. "*De nada*." He smiled, but there was no trace of warmth in it.

"Nothing to you, maybe, but—"

"I don't want to talk. Not to you, not to anybody. Nothing personal. I just don't want to talk."

"Can I buy you a drink?"

"Why? You don't owe me nothing. Do I look like I need a drink?"

Lex shook his head. "No, you don't. In fact, you like you had a couple too many already."

"Then why you want to buy me one? I don't want you to buy me a drink. I don't want nothing at all from you or anybody else. Just go away."

"You know those guys?"

Carlos nodded slowly, as if unsure whether to admit it. "*Sí*, I know them."

Lex sipped his beer. He wasn't willing to let it go just yet. He had a reason to sit there now, one that wouldn't call any undue attention to their conversation. If he let the chance slip, he might not get another. "You work around here?" he asked.

"Used to."

"Cowhand?"

"Sort of." Carlos took a long pull on his beer, then looked over Lex's shoulder for the barmaid. Catching her eye, he crooked a finger, then waited quietly for her to approach. He ordered two beers. Then he reached out to hook his fingers through the handles of both mugs and lifted them toward the barmaid. When she had left, Carlos said, "Amigo, I'm gonna buy you a beer. Then you are gonna get up and walk away from this table, *comprende*?"

Lex nodded. "I understand. Look, I'm not trying to make a pest of myself. You did me a favor and I'm just trying to thank you, that's all."

"No, señor, that's not all. I know who you are. And I know what you want. You think, because I am sitting here alone, because I am *borracho*, I will tell you things about Señor Schiller. But I don't have anything to say. Not to you, not to anybody. *Es verdad*."

"I won't lie to you, Carlos. You're partly right."

"It doesn't matter whether you lie to me. I know what I know. And nothing you know or want to know will make any difference to me. None. *Nada*."

"Fair enough."

The barmaid returned with two beers, set them on the table, and waited while Carlos fumbled in his pocket for money. He came up empty. Lex reached into his own pocket, paid the waitress, and pushed one of the mugs across the table.

Carlos smiled for the second time, this time with more warmth. "*Gracias.* You don't owe me nothing now. Okay? You feel better? Now we're even."

"Not quite, Carlos. I got to think my life is worth more than a glass of beer."

"Don't kid yourself, Señor Cranshaw. Around here, life isn't worth even that."

"What do you mean?"

"You know what I mean."

Rather than push it, Lex picked up his mug, took a sip, and sat back in his chair. Carlos drank his beer in four long swallows. He said nothing until the beer was gone. Then he stood up with exaggerated care. "Adios, Señor Cranshaw, adios."

"What are you going to do now?"

"Go back to work. As you saw, my pockets are empty. I need to work."

"Schiller won't keep you on."

Carlos spat. "I wouldn't work for him again, anyway. Even if he would have me."

"Then what? There can't be many places in these parts where you could find a job."

"Señor Kensington has offered me a job. The money

is not much, but"—he shrugged—"a man like me doesn't need too much anyhow."

"Watch your back, Carlos."

Carlos smiled again. "You see? Even you understand how things are. You watch your back, too, Señor Cranshaw. I am not the only one who should have eyes in the back of his head, eh?"

"You know Kensington had some trouble out at his place this morning?"

"Sí, I know that. This is a world of trouble, isn't it? There is no place a man can go where there is not some kind of trouble. A wise man picks what kind of trouble he wants. As long as he doesn't make any for anybody else, then he has done the best he can. God, perhaps, takes that into consideration, no?"

"For both our sakes, I hope you're right."

"You are not like me, Señor Cranshaw. You *will* make trouble. Soon, I think. And Señor Schiller knows that. Don't you think so?"

Carlos turned and walked on legs stiff as stilts toward the door. A moment later he was gone. Lex left the rest of his beer and went outside. In the hot sun, he could smell the dust from the street and the faint, sweetly rotten scent of fresh horse apples. Carlos was swinging into the saddle.

He looked at Lex for a second, snapped a crisp salute, and wheeled his mount. Lex watched him ride out of town, half expecting to hear the crack of a Winchester from one of the alleys. But by the time Carlos had reached the edge of town, nothing had happened. Soon the Mexican was a dwindling speck. He veered to the left and disappeared behind the last building on the edge of town.

Lex wondered where the wounded Roy had been taken. He decided to try Doc Kraus, since he wanted to speak to him anyway, and left his bay hitched in front of the Edelweiss. When he got to Kraus's office, the doctor was inside alone, woolgathering, his eyes fixed on someplace out beyond the moon. It looked to Lex as if Kraus could see right through the walls of the office.

"Doc, you got a minute?" Lex asked.

Kraus turned to him only slowly, and when he did, his eyes took a while to refocus. They shone unnaturally, as if they had been coated with glycerine. His speech was slow, and his lips and tongue had difficulty shaping the words. Lex noticed an empty bottle on the floor, but it was too small to be whiskey. He lowered himself into a chair. Kraus watched him without saying a word, his eyes bulging a little, as if he were turning into some kind of insect.

"What can I do for you, Mr. Cranshaw?"

"You have a wounded cowboy in here a little while ago? A man named Roy?"

"Roy Hankins?" The great head wobbled affirmatively. "Sure did. Unfortunately the bastard's gonna live. Just a graze. If that damn Muñoz would just lay off the hooch, there'd be one less rat scuttling around this dump."

"Muñoz?"

"*Ja*, Carlos. You were there. You saw it. Les Pardee told me so."

"Les Pardee... He a little man? Face like a brown whippet?"

"Weasel, Mr. Cranshaw. Les Pardee is a weasel. He looks like one and he is one." The doctor's head lolled drunkenly, like a boulder ready to topple from its perch. "Why are you pretending you know less than you do? You don't strike me as the kind of man to play games. Especially not with some poor old country doctor."

Lex didn't answer right away. He studied Kraus, trying to decide what was wrong. Baffled, he finally asked, "Are you all right, Doc?"

Kraus smiled. "Of course I am. Roy's all right, I'm all right, Carlos is all right. You're all right, too, aren't you, Mr. Cranshaw?"

Lex took a deep breath. He was about to ask another question when Kraus slumped to one side in his chair. His chest rose and fell as he breathed deeply, but he was dead to the world. Lex got up, walked over to the doctor's chair and retrieved the small bottle. He lifted it to his nose, sniffed it, recognized the sharp tang, then stuck his pinky in, moistened it with fluid from the bottom, and licked his fingertip.

He shook his head sadly.

"That's right, Mr. Cranshaw, laudanum."

He whirled around to see Anna Kraus, hands on hips, planted in the office doorway.

"How long?" he asked.

"Two years and three months tomorrow."

"Why?"

"Why does anyone get addicted to anything, Mr. Cranshaw? Weakness? A failure of nerve? Escape? All of them at once? I don't know."

"This has something to do with Clayton Schiller, doesn't it?"

Anna took a deep breath. She started to shake her head, but stopped. "I suppose so. In one way or another, everything that happens in Laidlaw has something to do with Clayton Schiller."

"You want to tell me how?"

"No, Mr. Cranshaw, I don't."

"Maybe you should reconsider."

"Maybe I should do a lot of things. But I have my hands full, Mr. Cranshaw. I can't do any more than I'm already doing. There is no room in my life for reconsideration of anything."

"You don't believe that, Anna." Lex took a step toward her.

She turned her back on him, and he expected her to bolt, but she stayed where she was, hugging her arms to her chest. She shook as if a sudden chill had hit her. He stepped closer, but she shook her head violently.

"No," she said, "don't come any closer."

"Anna, you have to let me help."

"You can't help. Nobody can."

"How do you know until somebody tries?"

14

LEX lay on the bed, his eyes wide, fixed on the ceiling. There was a slice of moon, and the pale light washed through the open curtains, just enough to paint the walls with shadow. His arm was mending, but not quickly enough to suit him. He hadn't felt this alone since the first few days after Rosalita died. That seemed so long ago, the memory made him feel like a very old man, older than anyone had ever been, older even than Methuselah. Older than the earth itself.

He chewed on his lower lip, trying to understand what was happening in Laidlaw. The town seemed to be falling down around the ears of its inhabitants. But each time he tried to get a grip on the problem, Rosalita's face would slide into view. He wondered whether it was some selfish streak in him, something that made him want to forget Laidlaw, forget Anna Kraus and James Kensington and Carlos Muñoz. He didn't want to believe that, but the temptation to wallow in his own sorrowful past was too great to resist.

He had never gotten over Rosalita's death. He wondered, if their son had lived, would things have been different. If Rosalita had lived, he knew they would have been different. He had been prepared to open himself up, to make room for the child, but there hadn't been time for that love to take root, so it was his wife he missed most.

And then he thought about another woman, one who had risked her life to save his. She had asked nothing in return. But he owed Miss Emily, owed her his life, and therefore owed her everything. He had never known her by any other name. She had saved his life when it would have been easy for her to walk right on by and leave him lying there in the muddy weeds at Shiloh, right where her son had found him. But she hadn't. She had taken him in, the last thing you'd expect a black woman to do for a Rebel soldier. But Miss Emily had seen beyond labels. He was a stranger, a wounded man whose life was seeping into the mud, and she had saved him.

And Miss Emily would not have turned away from Laidlaw. She would have done what was right, even if it cost her something. Could he do any less? The question echoed in the room as if someone he could not see were sitting there in the dark, whispering to him, daring him, challenging him to be as good as the woman who had saved his life.

And, drawing a deep breath, holding it, waiting for that sweet exhaustion to sweep over him, he knew he would try. He would try because he couldn't do anything else. What he was was all he had, and he was not about to turn his back on the cold, empty reality of that fact.

He swung his legs over the edge of the bed and walked to the window. Kneeling to rest his elbows on the sill, he stared out into the empty street. As far as he could see in either direction, not a single light burned in Laidlaw. It looked as if the people of the town had packed up and left without a sound. Here and there a curtain blew lazily in an open window, pushed by a hot wind swirling dust in the street. And even the wind was silent.

He could see Doc Kraus's place, as gray and still as the rest. As he watched, the front door opened, and a slim figure slipped outside. As the figure stepped out of the shadows, he recognized Anna Kraus. She crossed the street, turning her head to glance at her father's building, like a naughty schoolgirl slipping out after hours to meet a boyfriend.

Lex leaned farther out of the window to watch her until she stepped onto the boardwalk below and disappeared under the shingled ramada in front of the hotel. Curious, he listened for her footsteps on the walk, but heard nothing. It seemed as if the shadows had swallowed her up.

Backing away from the window and getting to his feet, he sat on the edge of the bed, wondering where Anna had gone. As if in response to the unspoken question, a soft knock sounded on the door to his room.

Lex moved quickly to the door and jerked it open. Anna was standing there in the hallway, her face shadowed by the wan orange light of a single lamp mounted on a sconce halfway down the hall.

"You're awake," she said.

He nodded. "Come in." Without waiting for an answer, he groped through the darkness toward the night table, fumbled with the lamp chimney while he fished a match out of his shirt pocket. The match flared, the sharp tang of phosphorous billowing out around the flame and making his nose twitch. The wick caught, spurted orange, then settled down to a pale yellow, a thin coil of black smoke swirling away from the descending chimney as Lex covered the lamp.

Anna was still standing in the doorway, one fist held to her chin, as if she were chewing on her fingernails. Her face was drawn, and she looked as if she had been crying.

"Come in," he said again, stepping toward her, reaching out with a hand and taking her by the elbow.

She seemed to topple forward, then stutter-stepped to regain her balance.

"What's wrong?" he asked. "Why aren't you at home, sleeping?"

She shook her head. He reached out, cupped her

chin in his right hand, and tilted her head back. In the lamplight, he could see the glittering traces of tears coursing down her cheeks, the drops like small liquid jewels that clung to her chin for a moment before losing their grip and falling free. He reached out with a thumb and caught one just before it broke lose. He smiled, trying to reassure her.

"What is it, Anna?"

She chewed her lower lip a moment, shook her head again, then looked at him. "It's Daddy."

"Is he hurt? What happened?"

"No, he's not hurt. Not yet. But..."

"Tell me, damn it!" he snapped.

"He's joined up with Mr. Kensington and some other men. That Mexican, the one who used to work for Clay Schiller, is one of them, and Ben Davis and Gunther Kleinhalder's brother, Erich. There are others, but I don't know who they are...."

Lex waited impatiently. "And...?" he coaxed. "What about them?"

"They're going to attack Schiller's ranch."

"When?"

"I don't know... soon. Later tonight, I think. I'm not sure." She started to cry in earnest then, partly out of fear for her father and partly, it seemed, out of shame that he would permit himself to get involved in something like that.

"You're sure about this?"

She nodded. "They had a meeting upstairs in the clinic. I heard them talking. Daddy wouldn't let me be there, but I sneaked up the stairs. I brought coffee, in case they heard me, and I just stayed there on the stairs and listened. I couldn't hear everything they said, but I heard enough to guess they're planning to do something foolish."

"Do you know why they were meeting?"

She nodded. "They know the sheriff won't do anything, and they're fed up. They don't think there's any other way."

"So a range war seems like a logical tactic to them, does it?"

Anna nodded again. "Kensington said Schiller had already started it. He said they had to protect themselves. They had to get rid of Schiller before anyone else got killed. Anyone but Schiller, Kensington said."

"And they think they can go toe to toe with Schiller's hired guns, do they?"

Anna shrugged. "I guess.... You've got to do something, Mr. Cranshaw. There must be something.... Can't you lock them up? Can't you stop them?"

"Where are they now?"

"Daddy's sleeping. The others have gone. He's supposed to meet them later."

"I can't lock them up. And I wouldn't if I could. That would just put them in Cannon's hands. That's the last place they ought to be. You want me to try to talk your father out of it? Do you think he'd listen to me?"

She shook her head. "No. You've got to stop them. You have to talk some sense into Mr. Kensington. He's the one who's pushing for this. The others won't do anything without him. If you can change his mind... This attack is wrong. I know it's wrong. Daddy knows it, too. They all know it, but they're frustrated and they're angry." Her voice trailed off, and she buried her face in her hands.

"They have a right to be angry."

Anna looked up sharply. "You mean you won't do anything to stop them?"

"I didn't say that, Anna."

"Then what did you mean?"

"I just meant that before you can stop a man from doing something, you have to understand why he wants to do it in the first place. I can hold these men at gunpoint, but that won't change anything. We can all sit in a room until we strangle on our own beards or until we're too feeble to walk, let alone use a gun. But that won't stop them from hating Schiller, from wanting revenge, or justice, and to these men, I'm not sure there's a difference. Hell, I'm not even sure there's a difference to me."

"So what will you do?"

"I could warn Schiller, but I don't think that would help. He's likely to take the offensive. He's got Cannon in his pocket, and he's got more men than he needs to take on a handful of vigilantes. Or I could ride for help, try to get some lawmen down here to keep the peace, maybe get Schiller arrested."

"Why don't you do that, then?"

"Because while I'm gone, there'll be nothing to stop Kensington from attacking Schiller. Or vice versa."

"I don't understand. It sounds as if you're telling me you can't do anything."

"I'm not sure I can, Anna. All I can do is try. Do you know where they intend to attack?"

"No."

"Can you find out?"

"I tried, but Daddy won't tell me."

Lex nodded slowly. "All right, I'll do what I can, but I can't promise anything, Anna."

"I understand."

Lex strapped on his gun belt, and looked at Anna. "You go on home."

"What are you going to do?"

"I'm going to get my horse saddled. Then I'll keep an eye on your father. I won't let him out of my sight. That much I can promise."

"Be careful, Mr. Cranshaw." She stopped then to look at him. "I'm sorry. I don't mean to be telling you what to do. I just..."

Lex smiled. "Sure you do."

She tried to return the smile. "Is it that bad? Don't answer that."

"I wouldn't think of it," Lex said. He moved to the door, opened it, then went back to the night table and blew out the lamp. In the darkness he could hear Anna's breathing. He wanted to tell her something, anything, to put her mind at ease, but there was nothing he could say that wouldn't be a lie. They were painted into a very tight corner. If there was a way out, Lex couldn't see it.

LEX had saddled his horse and was ready to ride in fifteen minutes. He moved the bay stallion outside behind the livery stable and hitched it to a splintered railing on a rickety stairway leading up to the second floor of the hotel. Then he walked down a dark alley toward the main street.

Keeping to the deep shadows, he was able to see the front of Doc Kraus's building, which was as black and lifeless as all the others in Laidlaw. He assumed Anna had made it back without waking her father. Checking his watch, he saw that it was nearly three o'clock. If the vigilantes were going to act before sunup, they would be making their move soon.

Lex sat and listened to the night. Crickets and locusts made a racket, responding to the heat. In the shadows behind him he could hear the skitter of tiny feet—mice or rats, probably—and once the yowl of a cat. It was nearly four before he heard the crunch of boots on the street. Inching forward, trying to keep his silhouette in the shadows, he saw two men moving toward the Kraus place.

Neither looked familiar. One man moved into the darkness alongside the clinic while the other tiptoed onto the boardwalk and tried the front door of the doctor's office. It was open, and swung inward with a shrill creak of hinges. The man ducked inside. Two minutes later a small flame flared in the front window, followed by the welling up of orange light from a coal-oil lamp.

The man reappeared in the doorway, then ducked around the corner. The light stayed on inside Kraus's office for a couple of minutes, then went out as suddenly as it had appeared. Seconds later the bulky figure of Heinrich Kraus appeared in the open doorway, peered up and down the street, then stepped out. The door closed, and Doc Kraus, carrying his boots in one hand and an old Springfield rifle in the other, tiptoed toward the end of the walk and vanished into the alley.

Lex waited just long enough to realize the horses must be behind the building, then darted out into the street, running on his toes. He skirted the walk, reached the end of the alley, and stopped. He had decided it would be better to follow the men and see what they were up to than to try to stop them before they got going. He couldn't watch them all, and they had time on their side.

He heard the creak of saddle leather then and leaned over to peer into the shadows. The moonlit sky at the other end of the alley was unbroken. Lex sprinted down the alley as the first clop of hooves echoed through the streets, not loud, and not hurried, as if the men wanted to make a silent getaway.

Stopping again at the end of the alley, Lex peered around the corner to see Kraus and his two visitors heading away from town. Lex raced back to his own horse, dimly conscious of the throbbing in his shoulder, and swung into the saddle. He pushed the bay down the alley, crossed the street, and headed into the narrow gap.

When Lex reached the other end of Kraus's building, he could just make out the three horsemen, grayed by the moonlight and distance, off to the west. They were swinging north now, and Lex fell in behind them. He couldn't afford to get too close, because the flat terrain made him too visible. Even a casual turn of the head might spot him.

The men weren't heading toward Clayton Schiller's spread, but they weren't heading toward the Kensington place, either. They had apparently arranged a rendezvous, probably at some central location. And they probably wanted to make sure they weren't seen together at Kensington's, in order to throw off Cannon's suspicion.

If anything happened to Schiller or any of his men, Kensington was certain to be among the first suspects. It was nearly four-thirty before a stand of cottonwoods broke the horizon, topping a gentle rise overlooking a creek that glittered in the moonlight. Lex was more than a half mile behind his quarry, and he couldn't afford to get much closer.

A small fire glowed among the cottonwoods, probably some kind of signal, since the night was too hot for the men to need its warmth. Lex watched the three horsemen ride up the hill and dismount. There was no cover at all that he could use, and he dismounted to cut down on the chance of being seen.

He couldn't risk riding closer, and he didn't want to leave the bay behind, in case the men left while he was too far from his horse. All he could do was sit and wait. It would be sunup in less than an hour. If the men were planning a night raid, they wouldn't be going too far.

The fire died suddenly, and as its light disappeared, Lex became conscious of the brightening gray of the sky. All he could see now was the dark bulk of the cottonwoods. There didn't appear to be any movement. Suddenly a gunshot cracked, its echo dying quickly. He had seen the muzzle flash of the gun, but the light was gone in an instant. He thought he could see the pale haze of gunsmoke drifting among the tree trunks, but he couldn't be sure. Then he heard hoofbeats.

The men were leaving, and as near as he could tell, they were riding down the far side of the hill. Lex sprang into the saddle and pushed the bay into a gallop. He charged across the valley floor, using the reins to goad his mount up the gentle rise. Cresting the hill, he reined in, skidded to a halt, and jumped from the saddle.

Running toward the cottonwoods with a drawn Colt, he found the still smoking remains of the small fire, but there was no other evidence that anyone had been there less than five minutes before.

Looking around in the dry grass, he found nothing, no spent shell, no body, nothing. He was at a loss to explain the gunshot, unless it had been an accidental discharge, but that seemed unlikely.

Running through the trees, he could just make out the dim shapes of several horsemen racing across the floor of the next valley. He hurried back to his horse, swung into the saddle, walked the bay through the trees, then dug his knees in. The horse spurted forward, its long legs pumping as it thundered down the far side of the hill.

It was getting lighter now, and he spotted something in the grass off to the left. It looked like a bundle of cloth. He slowed the bay and veered toward it. He was almost on top of it before he realized it was a man, face down in the tall, brittle grass.

Lex dismounted, letting the reins drag, and sprinted the last fifteen yards toward the motionless figure. He could see the dark smear of a bloodstain on the back of the man's shirt. The figure was large and vaguely familiar. Lex knelt and felt for a pulse. There was none. He rolled the body over onto its back.

Pete Cannon stared up at him, his eyes wide and motionless. The small entry wound in the shirt, just over the heart, was still bright with blood, and a thin trickle of bloody water coursed down over the sheriff's chin and jawbone, outlining them. Lex pushed his hat off, then leaned over and pressed an ear to Cannon's chest. The heart was still.

So, Lex thought, the vigilantes were serious, which was bad enough. But someone knew they were out, and that was worse. That was the only way to explain Cannon's presence there on the hillside. It wouldn't take much to turn Laidlaw into a battleground. Kensington might not have realized just how small a spark it took to start a prairie fire. But Clayton Schiller knew, and something told Lex it was already too late to stop it.

After covering Cannon with a blanket from his bedroll, he stared after the dim shapes of the horsemen for a second, then ran back to the bay. Vaulting into the saddle, he used his spurs for the first time. The bay exploded into a full gallop. Lex was less worried now about being seen. It was more important to get to Kensington and Kraus and the others before they attacked Schiller's men. Once that happened, Schiller would not be satisfied until the summer drought was slaked with blood, preferably that of sodbusters and small ranchers like James Kensington.

And that kind of conflagration would not spare foolish old men like Doc Kraus, no matter how noble their intentions or how great their provocation. As he galloped after the vigilantes, all he could see was the face of Anna Kraus, floating somewhere in the back of his skull like an accusing ghost. And the last thing Lex wanted was to have to tell her that he had been unable to save her father from himself.

The horsemen had already made the top of the next

hill and disappeared over the ridge. He couldn't tell if he was gaining on them or not. He debated riding straight to the Flying S, but even if Kensington had another destination in mind, it wouldn't make any difference. He had to stay on their trail, try to narrow the gap if he could, and put himself between the innocent but desperate men with blood already on their hands, and the greedy rancher.

It took him fifteen minutes to get close enough to see the vigilantes again. Cresting a hill, he saw them on a ridge about three miles ahead. He spurred the bay again, lashing him with the reins to get every bit of speed from the big stallion. He dropped down into the next valley as the vigilantes disappeared behind another hill.

Ten minutes later he was pushing up the slope on which he had seen the horsemen. Reaching the ridgeline, he saw a huge herd spread out in the vast, flat-bottomed valley ahead. Thousands of head of cattle drifted aimlessly in bunches, munching grass as they moved like an undulating tide.

Off to the left he spotted the horsemen. In the first light of dawn, he could count them now, nine of them. And at almost the same instant he spotted their destination. A pair of wagons, their canvas covers stained with years of trail dust and rain, sat under some tall pin oaks. A lariat remuda had been rigged among the trees. More than a dozen horses were inside it.

One of Schiller's crews, Lex thought. The night rider was nowhere to be seen. Lex hadn't heard a gunshot and couldn't explain why no one had been riding herd during the long summer night.

The horsemen charged down on the small work camp, spreading out as they drew closer to the trees. One of the hands, or maybe the cook, must have been awake, because a gun cracked from somewhere near the trees, and the charging riders fanned out even farther, their line breaking as some of the men, unused to gunplay, faltered, unsure what they should do.

Schiller's men were not similarly troubled. The gunshot had brought them spilling out of their bedrolls like angry ants, and a sharp volley, signaled by small white flowers blooming in a sudden bunch, was visible to Lex well before the crack of the gunfire reached him.

The vigilantes pulled back, one riderless horse bucking and then bolting back the way it had come. Lex charged hard, skirting the herd as closely as he dared. Schiller's hands were moving now, on foot, and the horsemen backed up. Lex knew what was going to happen. Schiller's men would give no quarter. This was the kind of thing they were used to, even enjoyed. One man alone would not be able to stop it. Lex reined in, yanked his Winchester and fired in the air again and again, until the magazine was empty. Then he drew his Colt.

The cattle were starting to move now, small groups bellowing and tossing their heads with every gunshot. When the Colt was empty, several hundred were already moving. After reloading as quickly as he could, Lex resumed firing. At the very least he hoped the stampeding cattle would distract Schiller's hands, and if he was really lucky, they might just cut between the vigilantes and the cowhands.

By emptying the Winchester again, he got enough steers on the move to do the trick. Then he rode along the outer edge of the stampeding herd. He could see the vigilantes turning their mounts half in fear of the stampede and half in terror of getting cut down by the Flying S hands.

Lex stayed with the herd until he reached the first of the terrified settlers.

"What in the hell is going on?" Lex demanded, as he reached out to snag one frightened man by his overalls and haul him from his mount.

The man turned on him, snarled something Lex didn't catch. He spotted Doc Kraus then and let the farmer go. "Doc," he shouted. But more and more cattle were joining the stampede, and Doc was cut off.

THE restless herd was beginning to get out of control now, hundreds of frightened cattle joining the small core Lex had frightened. He knew that the herd would run for hours, until it came up against an obstacle it couldn't swarm across, over, or around. Herds in full stampede had been known to plunge by the thousands off a bluff, piling body on body until the sheer weight of numbers crushed to death those who had survived the fall.

At least some of Schiller's men would have to tend to the herd, but Lex knew the settlers weren't in the clear yet. He rode up alongside James Kensington and grabbed him by the arm. Pointing to the riderless horse, Lex shouted, "Whose mount is this?"

Kensington, his eyes wide, his face distorted with range and fear, shook his head. "I don't know. Let go of my arm." He shook free and broke away from Lex, lashing at his horse with near frenzy. He seemed every bit as much out of control as the stampeding cattle.

"Where's Doc?" Lex shouted. But Kensington ignored him. He hadn't seen Kraus for fifteen minutes. Swept away from him by the surging tide of beeves, he had had to work his way in a great circle and come back around a second time.

Dust clogged the air, making it difficult to see. Thousands of hooves ripping and pounding the dry grass and drier soil underneath kicked up swirling masses of beige dirt. Between the thunder of the hooves and the bellowing of the cattle, it was all but impossible to hear.

Lex tied a kerchief over his mouth and pushed through the suffocating pall. He hadn't seen Doc Kraus and was starting to wonder if the riderless horse belonged to him.

Cupping his free hand around his mouth, he shouted again and again, "Doc? Doc Kraus? Doc, are you there?"

He thought he heard a faint cry, but couldn't be sure. A sudden rider loomed up ahead of him, and they nearly collided, Lex jerking the bay to one side at the last second. In the blinding swirl, it was impossible to tell friend from foe. Lex saw the Winchester pointing vaguely in his direction and ducked, just in case. But the rider, uncertain, didn't fire as he rode by.

More shapes, some clearly men on horseback, others stray cattle, boiled past him like logs in a swollen current. Shape and mass were all but indistinguishable from the choking shroud of dust that wrapped everything in its darkness.

Once more Lex cupped a hand to shout for Kraus.

He saw something then, off to the left. He saw the shadows of the trees, too, then the shape of one of the wagons. He was almost in the work camp. The cattle plunged in among the trees, the brown-backed tide parting like muddy water to skirt the cottonwoods, then linking up on the far side of the small stand.

Lex knew that if he went down, he would be trampled. Nothing could stop the herd, and he had all he could do to keep the horse on its outer edge. He heard a yell then, but couldn't tell what was being said.

In the overpowering fury of the stampede, words were ripped apart like so many worn rags, bits and pieces swirling in the air as directionless as the dust. Lex maneuvered in behind one of the wagons, getting the bay and the riderless horse out of the way of the cattle. Scattered gunshots seemed to come from every direction as Schiller's men tried to turn the herd, make it coil back on itself. If they could turn it, they could let it run itself out.

The worst of the thunder began to subside. The cattle rushing through the work camp were thinning out now, but the dust continued to choke the air. Lex slapped at the kerchief to free some of the dust clogging the fabric and making it even more difficult to breathe. He heard another shout, turned, but saw nothing at first. He could just make out the shape of the other wagon, fifteen or eighteen feet away. It looked like a squarish block of stone through the roiling dust.

Again a shout, this time clearly from the second wagon.

Cupping a hand over his mouth once more, he shouted "Doc? That you?"

"*Ja*, Herr Cranshaw."

"You all right?"

"I think maybe so. I've been shot." There was a long pause. "But it's not too bad."

"You hang on. This'll be over in a few minutes."

Lex waited patiently for the last stray steers to straggle by, then nudged his horse over toward the second wagon. The heavy dust was already beginning to sift out of the air. Everything was covered with a thick layer of the beige dirt, the particles so fine it felt like a smooth silk under the fingers.

Maneuvering in next to the wagon, he got Doc Kraus onto the back of the bay and rode out to the riderless mount. Kraus slid off the bay, and clapped Lex on the thigh. "Thank you," he said. "If you hadn't—"

"Forget about it, Doc. You did something stupid, but we'll talk about that later. It isn't over yet, and we'd better hope it ends before anybody else gets hurt."

As if to disabuse Lex of his optimism, a rifle cracked off in the distance, and a bullet whistled over his head, missing him by no more than a few inches. "Let's get out of here," he said, waiting for Kraus to mount up.

The doctor's left sleeve was bloodstained, and the tattered edges of thread where a bullet had plowed through the cloth were stiff with blood clotted with the fine dust. Doc managed to get into the saddle and let his left arm hang limply.

"Go on, get out of here," Lex shouted. He drew his Winchester from the boot and waited for Kraus to nudge his horse into motion, then turned to see where Schiller's men were.

Through the thinning cloud of dirt he could see several figures heading back toward the wagons.

Far across the valley floor, the thunder of the herd was a dull roar. It sounded as if the earth itself were shifting beneath their feet. Kraus pushed his horse into a gallop, and Lex waited for him to get a decent lead before turning to follow him.

As they rode out of the dust cloud, Lex was already closing the gap on the wounded physician. Far ahead, he spotted several horsemen, probably the rest of the vigilantes, milling about on a hilltop, uncertain whether to rejoin the fight or scamper home with their tails between their legs. Lex could only hope they would turn tail.

Glancing back over his shoulder, he saw a knot of Schiller's men racing after him. "Doc," he shouted, "get a move on. We're being followed."

Kraus turned, saw the pursuers, and kicked at his horse to urge it on. The first scattered gunshots crackled like burning timber, but none of the bullets came close. Lex fired once, just to keep the ranch hands honest, then spurred the bay into a full gallop. The vigilantes milling around up ahead seemed to realize what was happening.

Lex hoped they would stay where they were. If they came charging down the slope in some misguided sense of heroism, bloodshed would be unavoidable. They were still on the hill, more than a mile distant. Lex and Kraus had a long lead on Schiller's men, nearly five hundred yards. It was narrowing a little, but not much, almost as if the Flying S hands weren't sure they wanted to pursue.

Lex pulled even with Kraus and shouted to him. "No matter what I do, you keep going."

"Don't stop, Mr. Cranshaw. Please."

"You keep going, Doc, understand?"

Kraus nodded. "*Ja, Ich verstehe.*"

Lex slowed a bit then, thinking to throw a little lead toward the hands, just enough to slow them up and give Kraus a chance to catch up to Kensington and the others.

The men on the hill started down, and Lex waved his hands desperately, crossing them over his head, trying to signal that they should stay where they were. Three men came partway down the hill, then stopped, uncertain whether they should continue. The charging hands were firing sporadically, but the bullets were no threat at that range. At five hundred yards, on horseback, even a Winchester was not much of a threat.

Lex watched as Kraus slowly pulled away. The doctor kept looking back, as if trying to persuade Lex to follow him. When Kraus had a lead of a hundred yards, Lex swung in a circle, reined in, and brought the Winchester to bear. He fired three shots in quick succession. He saw the hands hesitate. They spread out a little, trying to get away from one another, as if a cluster would draw a bullet.

Looking back, Lex saw Kraus already reaching the bottom of the hill. The hands were only three hundred yards away now, but they had slowed down, none of them willing to be the first to come within range of Lex's carbine.

Lex fired once more, then again. He saw both bullets kick up gouts of sod and clouds of dust, but neither came within ten feet of the nearest horseman. He wheeled the bay then and broke for the hill. A distant shout drifted to him on the wind. He pushed the bay full out, turned to see the hands trying to recover their momentum, but the bay was fresh and was bigger and stronger than the cow ponies.

Kraus had caught up with the others now, and he was waving his arms to get them to push on. Lex reached the bottom of the hill. Bullets were slamming into the hillside all around him, none close. As the bay broke up the slope, Lex looked back again, He had regained his full five-hundred yard lead, and it was growing longer still.

The men above him were slowly moving over the ridgeline as Lex charged up the hill. As soon as he broke over the top of the hill, even a stray shot would pose no danger. He was on the ridge in seconds, glanced once more behind him, and saw one of the men—he thought it was Pardee, the little man from his visit to Schiller's—stand in the stirrups and angrily wave a clenched fist.

Plunging over the top, he saw Kraus and Kensington, rifles drawn, waiting for him at the bottom of the hill. The others had pushed on. Lex waved to them, and they turned their mounts and broke into a gallop. He caught them in a minute, spurting past as the bay's momentum carried him on by. They urged their mounts after him, and the three of them raced after the others. Lex was still furious at Kraus and even angrier at Kensington, but this was neither the time nor the place to let them know what was on his mind. There would be plenty of time for that.

They were nearly a thousand yards ahead of Schiller's men as the hands came over the top of the hill. Lex realized that they must have lain back, suspecting an ambush, because they were spread out in a long, ragged line and moving at a walk as they came over the ridge.

Kensington saw them and waved a hand triumphantly. "I guess we showed them we ain't afraid to go head to head with 'em, Doc," he said.

Kraus looked at Lex, who shook his head.

"You didn't show them anything, except how stupid you are," Lex snapped.

"Hell, we hit 'em head on. We didn't back down. Word of this gets around, and more folks'll be wanting to help us."

"You're wrong, Kensington. And Clay Schiller knows that better than you do. That's why he can't afford to let you get away with this. He'll be coming after you harder than ever. And I don't know where it'll stop."

"You worry too much, Cranshaw."

"We'll see about that."

ONCE they reached Kensington's spread, Lex read the men the riot act.

"You men are acting like a bunch of clowns," he said.

"You've taken the law into your own hands. You got Doc here shot up, and you could have gotten yourselves killed. This isn't the way to fight Clay Schiller. Kensington, I'm holding you responsible. I don't want to see a repetition of this incident. You hear?"

"And what choice do we have, Mr. High-and-Mighty Ranger? Are you going to go out there and take on Clay Schiller, Pardee, and the rest of them single-handed? Is that what you think? Because if you are, I'd pay good money to see that. I sure as hell would."

"No, of course not. But you don't handle a man like Schiller by reaching for your guns. You play right into his hands if you do that. That's what he *wants* you to do, for Christ's sake. Can't you see that? He's got you outmanned and outgunned."

"I see that half of my friends have already left Laidlaw County, that's what I see," Kensington said. "And the other half is busy packing up. Another month and there won't be anybody here *but* Clay Schiller. Is that the way it's supposed to be? I thought this was a free country. I thought Texas was supposed to be so big that it had room for everybody. Even a poor man like me, and Schliemann and Kleinhalder. I broke my back working my land. I built this goddamn house with my own hands. And there's not a man in this room who can't say the same thing. I didn't do that to sit back and watch it burn to the ground because some power hungry bastard decides he wants to play with matches. This is *my* land, dammit. And it's gonna stay my land if I have to cut Clay Schiller's throat with a pocketknife. I'll tell you one thing, Cranshaw: I won't leave."

"I'm not asking you to leave, Kensington. I'm not asking any of you to give up or to walk away from your land. I'm just asking you to be patient."

Kensington threw up his hands. "It's patience you want, is it? I've been patient, Cranshaw. I've stood by for going on two years and watched Clay Schiller tear this country apart and stick the pieces in his own damn pocket. Isn't that enough patience? How much patience should a man have to have? Is it enough when his barn's been put to the torch? Or does he have to wait for the damn house to burn down around his ears? Or maybe it's funerals you want. Is that it? Because we've had plenty of those, too. But I for one have gone to the last funeral I aim to."

Lex pounded his fist on the wall. Dishes rattled in the china closet, and a small ornate mirror bounced off the living room wall and shattered on the floor. Lex looked at the mirror, then at Kensington. "Sorry," he said.

"Look, Cranshaw," the farmer said, ignoring the damage, "I know you mean well, but well-meaning won't get the job done. It's guns we need. Lots of them. And men to pull the triggers. We wait much longer and there won't be enough of us. Then Schiller wins."

"I need a volunteer," Lex said.

"For what?" It was one of the others. He looked enough like Gunther Kleinhalder to be a relative.

"What's your name?" Lex asked.

"Erich Kleinhalder."

"Sorry about your brother," Lex said.

"*Ja*. Me, too. All of us in this room are sorry about Gunther. What do you want me to volunteer for?"

"I need someone to ride to the nearest telegraph station. Anybody know where that is?"

"I do," Kensington said. "It's over in Mitchell County. What are you planning? Gonna strangle Schiller with the wire? Is that it?"

The men laughed, but it was a bitter laugh, dry and brittle in the small room. Lex waited for them to quiet down before continuing. He understood their mood and knew how easily their bitterness could turn to fury... or to despair. And this was no time for either one.

"No, I need a message sent to Austin."

"Why don't you do it?" Kensington asked.

"Because I can't leave. Not now."

"We don't need you to take care of us, Cranshaw," Erich Kleinhalder said.

"Why don't you let Mr. Cranshaw speak, Erich?" Doc Kraus asked.

"Doc, you shouldn't have come along on this little hayride. No offense," Kensington said, "but you maybe should go on home and sit down with one a them little bottles of yours, don't you think?"

Kraus shook his head. "Damn you, Kensington, you have no business—"

"Cut it out," Lex shouted. "You won't get anywhere fighting among yourselves. That only makes it easier for Schiller."

"Seems to me like *you're* the one making it easier for Schiller. Tell us to put up our guns. Tell us to sit on our hands. Next thing you know, you'll tell us we can chase him off by throwing our property titles at him. That next on your agenda?" Kensington demanded.

Lex took a deep breath. "No, next is getting some help. Next is getting some more Rangers down here, men who know how to use their weapons, men who know how to handle gunfighters like Pardee and Roy and the others."

Carlos Muñoz was sitting quietly in a corner. He hadn't said a word since the meeting started. Now he got to his feet and walked to the center of the room. "Mr. Cranshaw is right," he said.

"What do you know about it, beaner?" Kensington snapped. "Hell, you were on Schiller's payroll until a couple of days ago."

"*Sí*, I was on his payroll. And that is very good for you."

Lex was intrigued. Kensington started to cut him off, but Lex raised a hand. "Let him finish," he said.

"I know some things about Mr. Schiller, about Pardee, about all of them. Things they've done..."

"You willing to testify in court, Carlos?" Lex asked.

Muñoz shrugged. "I have seen men like him before. In Mexico there are many, some who are much worse. The big rancheros, they were built the same way Señor Schiller is building his. The poor people—the campesinos, the peons—they get pushed out, and the rancheros grow like a fire spreading across the prairie. There is no way to slow them down, to stop them, because the *patróns*, they own the alcaldes, they own the governors and the mayors. The little people have no one to help them, no law to protect them."

"Ain't that what we got here? Wasn't it Clay Schiller put Pete Cannon in as sheriff? Don't he own Jim Cargill? Some mayor he is. Spends the whole damn day drinkin' in Schiller's saloon. Hell, Schiller owns the goddamn *law*, Carlos. You know that. It saved your own ass more than once, didn't it?"

Carlos shrugged. "*Sí*, it did that. But—"

"And it ain't no damn different now, Carlos. So you

might just as well go on back to Meh-hee-co."

Carlos glared at Kensington, but didn't respond. Lex jumped in before the argument could get even more personal. "Erich, will you go?"

Kleinhalder nodded his head. "*Ja*, I will go. What do you want me to say, and who do I send your message to?"

"I want you to send the message to Major Earl Podell in Austin. We need help, and lots of it, I think. I'll write everything out for you." To Kensington he said, "Do you have paper and a pencil?"

Kensington glared at him. "You think I'm illiterate just because I'm a farmer?" He stalked off, and Lex heard him rummaging around in another room. A few minutes later he was back, a couple of sheets of deckle-edged paper flapping angrily in one hand. In the other he held an inkpot and a pen. "This good enough?"

Lex nodded. "Thanks," he said, taking the paper and pen from the farmer's hands.

Lex went to a table and sat down. He'd been thinking about what to say, but now that the time was actually here, he wasn't sure. He scratched at the paper, reworked the message three times, and finally had something he could live with. After rewriting it on the second sheet of paper, he handed it to Kleinhalder. "How far do you have to go?"

The young immigrant shrugged. He looked at Kensington who said, "A hundred miles, pretty near. He's got to go all the way the hell to McMinn."

"How long will it take you?" Lex asked.

"I can ride there in one day. It will take another day to get back, if I get an answer right away. If it takes long for the answer, I don't know..."

"You better get started, Mr. Kleinhalder."

"*Ja*, I'll leave right away. You tell my sister-in-law, *bitte*?"

"We'll tell her, Erich," Kensington said. "You be careful. You want somebody to go with you?"

Kleinhalder shook his head. "*Nein* ... no, I'll be all right."

They all watched him leave, some of them doubtless thinking they'd seen him for the last time, others convinced he was on a fool's errand at best. When he was gone, Lex said, "I'm going to take Doc Kraus home. I'll be back in the morning. In the meantime, don't you do a goddamn thing, Kensington, you hear? The only thing I want you to do is to get Cannon's body into town."

"Let the son of a bitch rot out there. That's all he deserves."

Some of the others muttered among themselves. This was not the sort of thing they could ignore. A man deserved a decent burial.

"I'll give you a hand, Jim," Ben Davis said. "It ain't right to leave him like that."

"You bring him into town; then you come back here and stay here. Got it?" Lex said.

The farmer nodded. "I hear you. I ain't makin' any promises, though."

"You do as I say. I swear to God, you take the law into your own hands again and I'll see you behind bars. As it is, one of you men is responsible for the death of Pete Cannon. Whoever it is will have to pay for it."

"You arrest men for shooting skunks, too, do you, Cranshaw?" Kensington asked.

"I arrest men who break the law. In my book, murder's a crime."

"Maybe it was self-defense. You ever think of that?"

"That isn't up to me to decide. That's for the courts."

"You think we have a judge we can trust anywhere nearby? Or are you as dumb as you seem?"

Lex ignored the insult. "I'll be back at first light. You better be here. The rest of you, go on home. Meet me here in the morning."

The men muttered among themselves. "What for?" Kensington asked.

"We'll have to organize some sort of defense until the Rangers get here."

"You think we can afford to wait that long, you got another think coming. Schiller will be down here in two shakes, that pack of wolves with him. If I was you, Cranshaw, I'd sleep with one eye open and my finger on the trigger."

"Don't worry about me, Kensington. I can take care of myself."

The farmer snorted. "I ain't worried about you. I'm

worried about me and mine. That's all I got the strength to worry about."

"You cross me and you'll have one more thing to worry about."

18

DOC Kraus was silent on the ride home. He seemed ashamed of himself, but there was an undercurrent of anger in his embarrassment. Lex tried to draw him out, but Kraus kept shaking him off. Lex was worried about Kensington. The irate farmer definitely had a hot temper, and his volatility was a distinct liability.

Laidlaw was strangely quiet for noon. It seemed as if fewer horses than usual were hitched along the main street, and not a soul was outside. The empty chairs along both boardwalks gave mute testimony that something was wrong. Lex dismounted, then helped Doc Kraus out of the saddle. Anna stood in the doorway watching them, unwilling or unable to come down into the street. One hand went to her mouth when she saw her father's bloodstained sleeve, but still she stayed rooted to the sill, her other hand grabbing the doorframe so tightly Lex could see her knuckles whitened by the strain.

After helping Kraus up onto the walkway, Lex turned to look toward the sheriff's office. The door was open, and more than likely a deputy was on duty, probably expecting Pete Cannon, not knowing the sheriff's post was currently vacant.

Once Lex got the doctor inside, Anna seemed to regain her composure. "What happened?" she asked, directing her question to Lex rather than to her father.

"About what you figured. I got there in time this time, but I don't know how much longer we have before things get out of hand."

"Was anyone else hurt?"

"Cannon."

"Shot?"

Lex nodded. "Fatally."

Anna gasped. "Who . . . ?"

"I don't know. But I'll find out, I promise."

"I did it," Kraus said. "I killed him."

"Oh, Daddy . . . why?" Anna sank to her knees as Kraus lowered his bulk into a chair.

"He deserved it, Anna."

Lex wasn't so sure Kraus was telling the truth. The confession seemed too calm, almost proud, totally inconsistent with the doctor's manner. But for the moment, Lex had more important problems. Murder was murder, but when somebody took a notion to kill a crooked sheriff, you had to feel that just maybe there was good reason for it. That didn't make it right, but it made it understandable.

"I'll be back in a bit," Lex said.

Anna looked for all the world like a five-year-old child kneeling at her father's side. "Where are you going?"

"Somebody has to tell the deputy that Cannon's been killed."

"Who cares about that?" Doc said. "Nobody cares. Nobody gives a damn about anything in this hellhole. Look at this town, Mr. Cranshaw. Should anyone care what happens to it or to the people who live here?"

"Don't, Daddy, please don't."

"Anna, hush. Just get some water and bandages. We have to tend to my arm."

Lex left them on the edge of bickering, Anna frightened and confused, Doc angry and depressed.

The same surly deputy he'd met before was on duty. Lex touched the brim of his hat.

"Sheriff's not here," the deputy said, glaring at Lex. Now that the memory of Lex reaching across the desk had faded a bit, he was back to being as sullen as usual.

"He won't be, either," Lex said.

"What are you talking about? How do you know what he'll do?"

"Sheriff Cannon is dead. Somebody shot and killed him. Early this morning, I think."

"Who done it?"

Lex shrugged. "I don't rightly know."

"You're foolin' with me, ain't you? It ain't funny to

joke about something like that."

"I'm not joking. I found the body, but I didn't have time to bring him in. Kensington will bring him in later today. I'd have done it, but some of his friends were raising a bit of a rumpus, and that distracted me a little."

"What friends? What in hell are you jabbering about, Cranshaw?"

Lex waved off the questions. He told the deputy a few details about finding the sheriff's body, answered a couple more questions, then excused himself.

As Lex was moving toward the door, the deputy asked, "You didn't shoot him, did you, Cranshaw?"

Lex didn't bother to look back. He stepped outside and walked across the deserted street toward Kraus's. He found Anna in the kitchen, sitting at the table with her head in her hands. She didn't look up when Lex entered.

"Your father all right, Anna?" he asked.

She nodded, leaving her face buried in her open palms. Lex pulled up a chair and sat down across the table from her. "Anna, I know it's hard for you, but you'll just have to be strong for a little while longer."

She looked at him then, shaking her head slowly from side to side. "You don't believe Daddy shot Sheriff Cannon, do you? You can't believe that."

"I don't know what to believe, Anna. He was there when it happened. I know that. But I wasn't close enough to see who did it."

"He couldn't. He couldn't do something like that. You have to believe me."

"I want to, Anna. But right now what I believe doesn't really matter. Clayton Schiller is the problem. After we solve that, we can worry about other things."

"Suppose my father did kill the sheriff. What will happen to him? Will you arrest him?"

Lex waited a long time before answering. Finally, unable to give her the answer she so desperately wanted, he settled for the next best thing. "I don't know," he said. "I... don't worry about it."

"But he couldn't have done it. He hated Cannon, I know that. He was angry and... but not angry enough to do something like that. He's spent his whole life helping people. People who couldn't pay. People who mocked him for his accent when they didn't need him. People who could pay and didn't bother, because they knew he would never ask. Does that sound like the kind of man who could shoot someone in cold blood, Mr. Cranshaw? Does it?"

Lex shook his head. "No, it doesn't. But I've been a lawman for a long while, Anna. And in that time, if I've learned one thing, it's that you can never tell what a man might do if he gets desperate enough. Or if he feels he has no other choice."

"No. Not Daddy. You've got to believe me."

"You weren't there, Anna. I don't know what happened, but you don't either. All I know is what Doc told me. The sheriff is dead. I know that because I found the body. And your father says he did it. If he's lying, then... well, let's just say I'd like to know why he'd admit being guilty of a crime he didn't commit. That would take some real explaining."

He lapsed into silence. Pushing back the chair, he stood up. "I'm going to the hotel," he said. "I'll be there if you need me."

She looked him square in the eye then. "Now, why would I need you, Mr. Cranshaw? I don't need anyone who thinks my father is a murderer. I need someone who knows he isn't."

"I understand that, Anna. I do, but—"

"Never mind," she snapped. "Go on, get out. Don't worry about being disturbed. You're the last person I'd come to if I needed help."

Lex didn't bother to argue. At the moment there was no point in trying to get Anna to see his position. She was concerned about her father, probably too concerned to see things objectively, and rightly so. Doc Kraus was in trouble, whether or not he killed Pete Cannon. But she couldn't be expected to understand just how deep that trouble was.

In his own mind Lex was far from certain that Schiller could be stopped. It depended on too many things that were beyond one man's control. If Erich Kleinhalder got the message through, and if Earl Podell had men available, and if those men were able to get to Laidlaw before Schiller let his men loose in an orgy of violence, maybe things would work out. But that was three more maybe's than Lex wanted to contend with.

He went to his room and lay down. He took off his

gun belt, but set it on the bed next to him. He left his boots on and listened to the silence in the streets of Laidlaw. It reminded him of lazy summer evenings back in Kentucky, waiting for a thunderstorm. Only it wouldn't be water that would muddy the dusty streets of Laidlaw.

It was an hour later when he heard the hooves of a solitary horse. Each clop, muffled by the thick, sandy dust of the street, sounded like the dull tolling of a bell wrapped in a shroud. He walked to the window and watched the lone rider move lazily down the center of the street until he reached the sheriff's office, dismounted and tied off at the rail. The man went inside, and after ten minutes Lex knew he wouldn't be coming out.

He went back and lay down, once more letting the silence chew at him like a hungry worm. He fell asleep without wanting to and without having the energy to fight the waves of exhaustion washing over him one by one.

A knock on the door brought him to. It was dark outside, and when he sat up he could see the roofline of the buildings across the street. The rapping came again, and he started for the door, reaching back to grab his gun belt almost as an afterthought.

When he opened the door, he found Anna Kraus standing there, wringing her hands.

"What's wrong?" he asked.

She shook her head, then mutely extended a hand. When Lex closed it in his own, she pulled. He followed her, closing the door behind him. Anna was almost running by the time she reached the stairs. She kept jerking his arm, urging him to move faster and faster until he was taking the stairs two at a time.

When she reached the lobby, she let go of Lex's hand and started to run, nearly tripping as she raced through the door and out into the street. Lex broke into a sprint. He saw the door of the doctor's office yawning wide open, a dark hole in the gray facade, sucking in the moonlight as if it wanted to swallow it all.

"In here, quick!" Anna cried as she turned through the door to Doc Kraus's office. A single lamp, turned up high, sat on Kraus's desk. The doctor lay slumped on the floor. He was breathing shallowly, his mouth yawning open, his jaw slack. Doc's eyes were open, but they had an unnatural glitter in the lamplight, and they blinked with a strange slow motion that seemed almost artificial.

Lex noticed the small green glass bottle on the floor, scant inches from Kraus's hand. Anna reached out for the bottle, closing it in her long fingers but not moving it. It looked almost as if she wanted to pretend it wasn't there at all.

"Help me get him up," Lex said. "We have to keep him awake."

"This was an accident," Anna said.

Lex wasn't quite so sure. And he was beginning to wonder whether Doc might after all have been telling the truth about what had happened to Pete Cannon. He nodded.

"Don't worry about it now, Anna."

"It was an accident," she said again. She wanted desperately to believe it.

So did Lex.

19

LEX was up at dawn. As he walked out into the street, the sun was just peeking over the horizon, its swollen form that of a gigantic blood-sated tick creeping across the plains. He was carrying his Winchester, which he had kept in the hotel. He was more than a little surprised that the night had been, if not peaceful, then at least quiet.

The ride out to Kensington's took him a little better than a half hour. It seemed clear that Kensington was the linchpin. It also seemed likely that Schiller understood that. It was Kensington who had instigated the attack on Schiller's work camp. It was Kensington who had defied Schiller's men and beaten back the attack on his home. It was logical to conclude, then, that it was Kensington that Schiller would go after.

The other men had been drawn to the farmer, collected around him like school kids around an admired teacher. Kensington had stood up to Schiller, something the others had been unable or unwilling to do. That made him attractive to the more fearful among them. They would be willing to follow him, but just so far. Schiller almost certainly knew that. Kensington's resistance was the last obstacle to Schiller's total domination of Laidlaw County. Get rid of the defiant farmer and the county would be his. The others would fold up like an accordion, moan one last breath as the bellows exhaled one final time, and it would be all over.

Lex rode harder and harder, the closer he got. He half expected to hear the sound of gunfire drifting toward him on the morning air. But the plains were deathly still. The sky was a perfect blue; not a cloud marred its infinite expanse in every direction. It was empty even of birds, except for a solitary hawk drifting high above him on the currents of rising air.

He wondered how Anna had fared. He wondered whether Doc Kraus was still alive. It troubled him that he had caved in to her so easily, had run like a scalded cat when she commanded him to leave. And then, when the doctor was almost unconscious, he had not known how to deal with her. She was strong, as strong as her father was weak. But that strength was nearly played out. He could see it in her eyes, their haunted dance unable to linger on any one thing. He could see it, too, in the sag of her shoulders, the drawn features, even in her walk, which had lost its spring, as if the suppleness of her body had suddenly deserted her.

But the problem was bigger than Anna. There were too many lives, too many families, at stake to let his affection for one woman interfere with what he had to do. At times like this, he missed Rosalita more than ever. And he recognized that whatever attracted him to a woman like Anna would not withstand the demands of his job. He could not afford to get attached. That kind of connection was a millstone, and it would take only one, just a single hesitation under the gun, a single miscalculation for reasons of the heart, to crush him under its weight. And no one could save him then.

When the Kensington place came into view, it looked small, smaller than he remembered. What was it, he wondered, in the mind of a man like Clay Schiller that felt diminished at the sight of a James Kensington? How could a man with so much want still more, want it all, even to the point of begrudging a man like Kensington his tiny patch of earth?

Maybe it was fear. Maybe the Kensingtons of the world reminded the Schillers of their own roots, their own tiny stature in so big a world. Maybe in driving off the Kensingtons, they were driving away memories of who they were and where they had come from. It was understandable, but unacceptable.

Several horses, all saddled, were hitched to a lariat strung between two trees. As he drew near the house, he spotted Carlos Muñoz lounging on the front porch, his hat tilted forward a bit as if he was napping. But as Lex dismounted, he noticed the black eyes fixed on him. Muñoz said nothing until Lex tied off. Then he got to his feet and stepped off the porch.

Taking Lex by the arm, he pulled him off toward the trees. "We have to talk, Señor Cranshaw," he said.

"What about?"

"Many things. First, the doctor. He didn't shoot the sheriff. I did." Muñzor stared at Lex, daring him to say something.

Lex just nodded.

"The doctor knows it was me, and he is trying to help me. He doesn't understand that I don't care. When this is over, I will go back to Mexico, if you permit me. If not..." He shrugged.

"No promises, Carlos."

Muñoz shrugged again. Lex waited. It was obvious that the Mexican wanted to say something else.

Carlos looked up at the trees. The leaves had begun to stir in a stiff breeze. They hissed as the branches swayed. When he spoke again, Carlos had to raise his voice a little to make certain he could be heard.

"I have done some things... things for Señor Schiller. I know some things, too, that others have done, always on orders from Señor Schiller." He stopped, looked at Lex for a long moment, then shrugged his shoulders in a gesture of helplessness. "I will tell the judge what I know, if..."

"You want assurances, is that it? You want me to tell you that you won't be held responsible?"

"No, señor. A man is always responsible. It doesn't matter what the judges say, or the juries. I am responsible for what I did. I just want... I guess... I want to make a confession, not like in a trial, but like in church. I want to make my peace with God, señor."

"I can't help you with that, Carlos. That's got to be up to you and the Almighty."

"I understand that, Señor Cranshaw. I have been doing much thinking. Ever since that day in the saloon. I didn't know why I did what I did. But I had been thinking much about it. Always at night I would lie awake for hours. I was there in the bunkhouse, Señor Schiller's bunkhouse. I was taking his money, eating the food he provided for me. The roof over my head belonged to him. I couldn't stay there anymore. I knew that. But leaving was not the answer, not the whole answer. I had to try to make things right. I can't..." He choked up then and turned his back.

Lex clapped a hand on the Mexican's shoulder. "It's a hard thing you are doing, Carlos. Very hard. I understand just how difficult it must be for you. I can't make any promises, but I'll do what I can."

Carlos nodded without turning around. "We will talk more later," he said. "I have to think more, to get things straight in my head. I—"

He didn't get to finish. The explosion of gunfire from the far side of the house drowned out his last words. Lex spun on his heels. He could see the wave of riders sweeping up over the hill from the far side. "Come on," he shouted.

Carlos broke into a run for the house. He was faster than Lex and reached the house first. Lex stopped just long enough to grab his carbine from its boot, then ducked around the corner of the house. There must have been twenty men, maybe more. They were dismounting now, dropping to the ground on the hilltop, which gave them a good view of the Kensington house.

It was long range, but their position was secure, and the men in the house would have a hard time moving. The riders would be able to cut them to pieces if they tried to leave, and if they stayed inside, it would just be a matter of time before the siege broke them.

Lex sprinted along the front of the house and ducked inside. "Carlos," he shouted. "Carlos!"

The Mexican had already taken up a position inside the house at one of the windows.

"What are we going to do, Cranshaw?" Kensington shouted. "There must be a hundred of them."

Lex glanced around. "Where's your wife and kids?"

"I sent my wife and them to her sister's," Kensington said.

"Put a man in every window. Don't go outside. Carlos and I will slip out the front before they encircle the house. It's our only chance. And there's nowhere near a hundred of them, Kensington."

"They'll cut you to ribbons."

"Not if we're careful. Carlos, you have any extra ammunition?"

Muñoz nodded. "Sí, in my saddlebags."

"All right, let's go, then."

Lex and Carlos left by the front door and sprinted away from the house, angling toward some trees off beyond where the barn used to stand. Someone spotted them, and a volley whistled around them, bullets whistling past and ripping hunks of bark from the tree trunks. Carlos stumbled, scampered several feet on hands and knees, then collapsed against the base of a cottonwood.

"You all right?" Lex shouted.

"Sí, I'm all right."

Already they had succeeded in dividing the attackers' attention. Four men split off from the main band and started toward the trees, one man firing for cover while three advanced.

"Get the cover man," Lex shouted. He drew a bead on the lead runner with his carbine. He fired once, narrowly missed, but came close enough to send the man sprawling, then jacked a second shell into the chamber.

Carlos sighted in on the cover man with his own Winchester, fired twice, and sent the rifleman sprawling. The wounded man rolled onto his back and started to push himself back up the hill with his bootheels. Lex took aim on another of the advance men, but they had gotten cautious and were lying flat in the tall grass. Only their hats stuck up over the grass.

But that was enough.

Lex fired again, saw one of the hats sink out of sight, and turned his attention to the wounded man scrambling up the hill. He was almost within reach of a clump of forsythia, its bright yellow-green leaves waving in the wind. Lex fired again, and the man howled in pain, then grabbed his leg just above the knee.

The remaining attackers were pouring continuous fire into the house, but men inside were conserving their ammunition. It sounded as if only one man at a time was returning fire, and then only when he had a reasonable chance of hitting something.

Carlos moved out beyond the cottonwoods, trying to get a glimpse of the last of the four men who had split off from the others. He sighted one in the grass just below the crown of a Stetson sticking up a couple of inches. The Winchester cracked, and the hat went flying, but it seemed as if the man had managed to slip away, leaving the Stetson behind as a decoy.

The rest of the attackers were slowly fanning out. Lex spotted two men out beyond the far corner of the house. From his angle, it appeared that they might not be visible to the men inside. If they managed to get near the house without being seen, the defenders would be in trouble.

So far he hadn't seen Pardee or Roy. He wondered if Schiller himself would show up. Knowing that he had to break the back of the small ranchers now or run the risk of losing everything he had tried to build, he might make an appearance. Schiller didn't seem that concerned about his reputation, perhaps because no one yet claimed to have seen him pull a trigger himself.

But that was for worrying later. Right now Lex had to do something about the two men sneaking up on the house.

"Carlos," he shouted.

The Mexican was on the far side of the trees, and Lex couldn't see him. He wanted Muñoz to cover him before he made a move toward the house to head off the two men sneaking down the hill. He couldn't afford to turn his back on the one man still out there somewhere in the tall grass.

Sprinting through the trees, keeping low and zigzagging, using the cottonwood trunks for cover, he reached the open grassland on the far side just as the missing man rose up out of the weeds. He was just ten feet behind Muñoz, whose back was turned.

Lex fired at the same instant he shouted to warn Muñoz.

The Mexican turned as the gunman went down. Muñoz looked at the wounded man in the grass, walked toward him, and reached down to snatch the man's gun away as the gunman writhed in pain, his shoulder bleeding heavily.

Carlos tucked the man's gun into his belt and smiled. "Now we're *really* even, eh, amigo?"

LEX reached the house, skidded to a halt, and stopped. Moving to the first window, he whispered, "It's me, Cranshaw."

Ben Davis, another farmer, leaned out the window, his black handlebar mustache glazed with sweat. "You scared the bejesus out of me, Cranshaw. Good Christ, man, don't be sneaking up on people like that. I'm a farmer, I ain't no gunfighter."

"Tell Kensington two men are off the right front corner of the house, in the tall grass. Carlos and I are going to try to get to them before they come any closer."

Davis nodded. "You want us to do anything?"

"Not now. We'll see what happens. To get at them, we're going to have to move past the windows on the far side. I don't want to get shot in the back. Make damn sure everybody knows what's going on."

Davis nodded. He started to pull his head back, then stopped. "We gonna make it, Cranshaw? Can we pull this off, or are we just spittin' in the wind?"

Lex smiled. "We'll pull it off, Mr. Davis."

The farmer tried to grin back.

"And if we don't," Lex said, "we won't be around to worry about it much."

"Should have kept my damn mouth shut. My wife is always telling me that, but I never learn." This time he managed a genuine smile.

Carlos slid in behind Lex as Davis moved inside to tell Kensington what was about to happen. "I'll go," he said.

"No need, Carlos. I can handle it."

"Then we'll both go. I got some to make up, no? This is partly my fault."

"Don't worry about it, Carlos. We'll hash that out later, all right?"

The Mexican nodded. He moved to the far corner of the house, dropped to one knee, and peered around the corner as Lex moved in behind him.

"See anything?" Lex asked.

Carlos shook his head. Pointing toward some cottonwoods across the hillside, he said. "If we can get to them trees, we have a better chance. They'll give us some cover, and we can see the whole front of the house from there."

Lex looked doubtful. "I don't know," he said. "That's a long run. We'll be sitting ducks. All the way across the hill, there's no place to hide."

"That's why they won't expect us to try," Carlos said. "That's why we can make it, but we have to go together. They'll probably spot us once we make the break, but it'll be too late. But if just one of us goes, they'll be waiting for the next man."

Lex moved past Carlos. "I'll take the point," he said. "I'll count to three, then run like hell."

He glanced back at Carlos, who was just getting up off his knee. "Whatever happens," Carlos said. "Nobody stops. If one of us gets hit, the other keeps going."

"Understood," Lex said. "Ready?" Carlos nodded, and Lex began to count. "One... two... three!" He broke into the open, his heels pounding on the dry sod. The tall grass was stiff and clawed at his legs, wrapping itself around his ankles and slowing him down. He kicked high, trying to compensate. The sprint was less than a hundred yards, but the trees looked as if they were a mile away.

He could hear Carlos slashing through the grass behind him. Keeping one eye uphill, he searched for the hidden gunmen, but saw no sign. Someone shouted then, and two men near the ridgeline rose up on their knees and opened fire. The men in the house opened up, trying to provide cover. One of Schiller's hands pitched forward and disappeared in the tall grass. Bullets were clipping the grass all around him as more of the besiegers opened fire.

Lex was still thirty yards from the cottonwoods when he heard a groan and turned to see Carlos stumble, then fall. The Mexican flailed his arms, signaling for him to keep going, but Lex stopped in his tracks, then turned and fired up the hill, leaving one round in his Colt. He tossed the Winchester into the trees and started back for Carlos.

The Mexican was already scrambling forward, but he was hurt, and his progress was hampered by the tall grass. Lex reached him as he tried for the third time to get up. His left leg was bleeding heavily. A through-and-through wound, it looked like. The Mexican winced as he tried to put his weight on the wounded leg.

Lex grabbed him around the waist. "You shoot and I'll run," he said.

Carlos nodded, clamping his teeth over his lower lip to take the pain. They started forward, the smaller man dangling under Lex's good arm. He heard a crack, then another right behind him, as Carlos fired his revolver, trying to buy them some time. A shout sounded behind them, back near the house.

Lex turned to see Ben Davis on both knees, just past the back corner of the house, firing a carbine up toward the ridgeline. The farmer was making no attempt to aim, substituting fury and frequency for marksmanship.

Lex struggled toward the trees, aware that every second in the open was like a year off his life. One second too long and his life would be over.

The trees seemed to back away from him. Carlos fired the last round in his Colt, then reached for Lex's pistol. "Only one round," Lex grunted. The grass snaked around his ankles, and, unable to kick as high with Carlos draped around him, he lost his balance and fell heavily, the Mexican landing in a heap right beside him.

The grass around them was tall enough to give them some protection, but there was nothing on the hillside that would stop a bullet except the distant trees. While Carlos ripped a sleeve off his shirt and knotted it around his wounds, Lex broke the Colt open and reloaded, pressing himself flat and fumbling for the bullets while trying to keep one eye on the slope.

Finished with the makeshift bandage, Carlos reloaded his own pistol. "You all right, amigo?" he asked.

Lex nodded. "So far. But we got a long way to go yet."

"I told you not to come back, didn't I? Now they know where we are, it will be much harder."

"Maybe not," Lex said. Glancing across the hillside, he saw the scorched ground where the grass had burned off a few days before. Below them, the ground was all bare earth and charred stubble.

Carlos saw where he was looking. "Good idea," he said. "You got a match?"

"Sure do. But we got to get down the slope a bit. I don't want to burn us to death, just kick up a lot of smoke."

Carlos grinned. "I can get myself down there," he said. No sooner had he finished speaking than he started to roll down the hillside, his arms extended over his head, the Colt gripped tightly in one hand. His uncertain progress crushed a swath of the tall grass nearly seven feet wide, its edges broken and less regular where his arms and legs had put less weight on the brittle blades.

Ben Davis was continuing to fire randomly up the hill while Kensington and the others in the house were banging away sporadically. Lex crawled down the swath of broken grass and felt like a shuttle in a loom rushing toward an uncertain fate.

When he reached the edge of the burned patch, he fished a couple of matches out of his pockets, handed one to Carlos, and then moved toward the trees a few yards. When he was far enough away, he nodded, then flicked the match head and cupped the flame in his palms. Carlos did the same, then touched his match to the grass and started to roll toward Lex. Lex lit his own patch and started crawling.

Already the dark gray smoke from Carlos's fire was beginning to thicken and spread out. The burning grass crackled and sizzled, and insects, almost as brittle as the grass itself, swarmed up and away from the heat and smoke to hover in a thickening cloud above them. Lex was moving as quickly as he could without outstripping the cover offered by the thick smoke.

On the hillside above him, he knew, more than a dozen men were strung out, and somewhere farther down, two more men were trying to get to the house. He was puzzled by that move, but it was more important to stop their advance then to figure it out. Or was it?

He was almost to the trees now, and Carlos, hauling his injured leg behind him, was pulling himself painfully forward. The Mexican was a game one, Lex thought, and wished there was something he could do to help him. In the back of his mind was the gnawing suspicion that Carlos had yet to reveal the full extent of his services for Clayton Schiller, and the list was certain to be unsavory, at the very least.

The grass was burning uphill, tongues of flame licking out ahead of the ragged line. The smoke was hanging in the air and beginning to obscure the hilltop. Setting the blaze was a calculated risk. It was the only way to cover his advance to the cottonwood stand, but it made Schiller's men every bit as difficult to see.

While he waited for Carlos to cover the last ten yards, Lex retrieved his carbine and peered through the haze, looking for any sign of the two men who had been trying to get close to the house. He had almost given up when he saw a shadow, not as close to the house as he had been looking. The man shot straight up, and Lex could tell he was too far to the side to be seen from either of the front windows. The side windows afforded a glimpse of him, but so far no one in the house seemed to have realized he was there.

The man fumbled with something waist high, but Lex wasn't able to see what it was. The man brought his right arm back, then raised it overhead. Lex saw the strange light, sparkling and winking, and it took him a second to realize what it was. By then, the arm had already come forward. The object arced high overhead, tumbling end over end as it flew toward the corner of the house.

The abrupt clap of thunder told everyone inside the house what Lex already knew—dynamite. The second man stood now, his stick of explosive already lit. Lex aimed and fired just as the man's arm started to move forward. The dark cylinder in the man's hand went almost straight up as the cowhand, staggered by the impact of the bullet, let the dynamite go too soon. It spiraled high overhead, then tumbled back down not ten feet from the wounded man.

The man limped away, doubled over and holding his chest, stumbled once, and then fell forward on his face. The fall probably saved his life, as the second stick of dynamite went off. A cone of dust and smoke spewed upward, and grass funneled out and away from the blast in every direction. Lex could see the hole in the grass like the mouth of a green volcano, still spitting smoke and dust, or yawning wide to suck it all back in.

Carlos looked at him. Lex shook his head. "I don't know," he said.

The first man scrambled through the grass, sprinting now, toward the corner of the house. The men inside must all have hit the floor, because not a single shot cracked from any of the windows. Lex drew a bead on the running man, lost him through the haze for a moment, then picked him up again, not thirty feet from the house.

This time, it looked as if he wanted to throw the explosive into the building. Lex aimed and fired, but missed. He saw the bullet spang off the wooden window frame, leaving a pale scar, barely noticeable through the dense smoke. The next shot slammed into the running man's shoulder and sent him sprawling. Lex looked for the explosive and didn't see it. The man was yelling then and trying to get to his feet, but in his panic, his legs refused to work for him, and he began to roll. He slammed into the side of the house, then tried to crawl up the wall.

When the dynamite went off, the man disappeared behind the column of smoke. And when the smoke cleared, he was nowhere to be seen.

For a long moment there was silence, as if both sides had been deafened by the blast or stunned into immobility. Then, almost as if on signal, a furious volley crackled across the ridge as Schiller's men resumed their assault.

"You stay here," Lex said, grabbing his Winchester.

"Where are you going?" Carlos demanded.

"Just cover me."

Lex had just ducked into the smoke, uphill from the advancing flame, when he saw two more men ride over the crest of the hill.

One was Pardee.

The other was Clayton Schiller.

CLAYTON Schiller sat on his horse with a haughty disdain for stray bullets, as if he thought himself a worthy successor to Stonewall Jackson. He surveyed the hillside, half a dozen of his men strewn like war dead across the slope, his hands draped across the pommel of his saddle, the reins resting loosely in his curved fingers.

Pardee stayed on his own mount slightly behind Schiller, but the little man looked nervous, as if things had gone somehow wrong in a way he couldn't quite identify or understand. Schiller turned to him, said something Lex couldn't hear, and Pardee dismounted, swatted his mount, and sent it loping back down the hill and out of sight.

"Cranshaw," Schiller shouted. "I know you're down there somewhere. Come on out. We have to talk."

Lex watched as Pardee moved across the hillside, then lay down in the tall grass and became all but invisible. He saw something glint in the sunlight, probably a rifle barrel, but Lex couldn't be certain; Pardee had not drawn a rifle from his scabbard before spanking his mount away.

"Cranshaw, you down there? You hear me, boy?"

Lex debated answering, then decided against it. He wanted to let Schiller stew a little in his own juice. Answering the man would be too much like admitting that he was in charge. As long as Schiller believed he had the upper hand, he'd be hard to deal with. It would be interesting, at least, to watch him sweat a little—if he could be made to sweat, which was far from certain.

And in the back of Lex's mind was the thought that Erich Kleinhalder was out there somewhere, maybe already on his way back. And maybe Erich had gotten through to Podell. With any luck, a detachment of Rangers might already be on the way to Laidlaw. It was a slim hope, but a drowning man doesn't take calipers to measure the straws.

Carlos crept in beside Lex. "Don't you go out there, amigo," he said. "Don't trust him, no matter what he says. He'll promise you anything to get you out in the open. Then—"

"My mama didn't raise no fools, Carlos," Lex whispered back. "If I go out there, it'll be because I have a good reason. So far, he hasn't given me one."

"He will, but it'll be the last good reason you ever hear," Carlos warned.

Once more Schiller bellowed, this time changing his target. "Kensington, you down there?"

A rifle cracked from a far window, and the bullet sailed high and wide. Schiller never moved a muscle. "I thought so," Schiller said. "I got an offer for you, Kensington."

Another shot broke the stillness, and a third, its sharp report drowning the echo of the preceding shot.

"Get off my land, Schiller," Kensington bellowed.

"It's not your land, Kensington. You know that as well as I do."

"The hell it ain't. I sweated for it. I built this place with my own hands. I ain't about to let you run me off."

"You don't have a chance, Kensington. You know that. But I'm a reasonable man. I'll make you an offer. I'm willing to buy your place. I'll give you top dollar. Under the circumstances."

"What circumstances are those, you greedy bastard?"

"It ain't often a man like me is willing to pay for something that's rightfully his already. But I'll make an exception this time."

Kensington didn't answer right away. When he did, it was apparent that Schiller had piqued his interest. "Why?"

"Because I'm a reasonable man. And I believe you are, too. I don't want trouble. It's not necessary. I just want you off my land."

"I already told you, it ain't your land."

"I can run you off, dammit."

"You ain't had much luck so far, have you?"

"Come on, James, you know I haven't half tried yet. You really think you can stand up to me? I have sixty men, and most of them aren't even here, because I don't need them. But I don't want bloodshed if it can be avoided."

"You tell that to Gunther Kleinhalder's widow, Schiller. Tell it to Karl Schliemann. Hell, you know the names as well as I do."

"You're on your own, Kensington, you realize that, don't you? Cranshaw's gone. He can't help you. And that pathetic bunch of sodbusters in there with you can't help. Now I'm going to say it one more time: you come on out, we'll talk it over, and I'll pay you a fair price; you stay there and there's only one way it can end. You know that."

"How much?"

"Come on out. We'll talk about it."

"Don't do it," Lex whispered. He couldn't believe the farmer would be that stupid. But he knew Kensington was desperate. Schiller's offer for a peaceful solution had to be tempting.

He looked for Pardee, but didn't see him. "Carlos," he whispered, "where's Pardee? You see him?"

Carlos shook his head. "We can take Señor Schiller from here, though. Then it is all over, no?"

"No. I want him alive, if I can manage it."

"You are making a mistake, Señor Cranshaw. The man is a snake. Kill him and you'll do everybody a favor."

"Not that way, Carlos. And don't you go getting any

ideas, either. You hear me?"

Carlos nodded. "But I think you should listen to me."

"Schiller's in the business of back-shooting, Carlos. But I'm not. I'll take him the right way or not at all."

Lex grabbed his Winchester and started back through the trees.

"Where are you going?" Carlos whispered.

"I have to get near the top of the hill. Pardee's out there somewhere, and if Kensington is fool enough to come out, I know what's going to happen. So do you."

"There's nothing you can do about it, Señor Cranshaw. We have to hope Señor Kensington is not the fool we know he is."

Lex slipped away through the trees, the Mexican's words echoing in his head. The cottonwoods would cover him for all but the last thirty yards to the hilltop. If he could get on a level with Schiller or, better yet, a little higher, he could look down on the Kensington place and just maybe spot where Pardee was hiding.

Kensington had said nothing further, and Schiller, sensing that he had said as much as he ought to, let the silence lengthen. He knew the pressure was on Kensington, and the longer he had to think about things, the more the pressure would work on his judgment.

By the time Lex had reached the last clump of trees, nearly four minutes had passed. Not a shot had been fired, not a word spoken. Glancing down the hill, he saw something that made his blood run cold. A white flag was being waved from the far corner of the house. No one was visible beyond it, but there was no doubt that someone in the house was coming out. It had to be Kensington.

Where the hell was Pardee? Lex scanned the hill from side to side, but there was no trace of the little man. The flag had stopped waving, and now a man could be seen in profile, just slipping out from behind the back corner of the house.

"Hold your fire, Schiller. I'm coming out."

Lex half expected Schiller to burst into laughter, but the rancher was too skilled a bluffer to give himself away. Kensington was already moving up the hill, keeping to the side of the house. He was pressed flat against the wall, the white flag fixed to the barrel of his Winchester. The white cloth hung limp, its end just barely above the brim of Kensington's hat. "Dammit!" Lex muttered. He watched helplessly as Kensington gingerly crept toward the front corner of the house. He couldn't shout for the farmer to go back without giving his own position away. That would have been suicide. With both the Ranger and the farmer in the open, Schiller would give the word and both of them would be cut to ribbons.

Lex sprinted toward the top of the hill now, conscious that any noise might betray him.

He had almost reached the crest when he heard the shout. It was Carlos.

"Señor Schiller," the Mexican hollered.

Lex turned then and saw the look of surprise on Schiller's face. He could just see Carlos at the front edge of the line of cottonwoods.

What the hell is he trying to do? Lex wondered. It

wasn't until Schiller made the next move that he understood.

"Pardee, you see him?" Schiller shouted.

The reply was a rifle shot. The bullet slammed into a cottonwood trunk not an inch away from where Carlos had been. The Mexican had ducked out of sight, but he had done what he set out to do. Lex spotted Pardee, as Carlos had known he would. Dropping to one knee, he sighted in and aimed. But he couldn't pull the trigger. Not yet.

"Put it down, Pardee," Lex shouted. "And stand up with your hands over your head."

Schiller had dismounted, and now he turned in his tracks. Like a flash, he went for his gun. Lex saw it, warned him off with a shot that slammed into the dirt just inches from the rancher's feet. Staring at Lex, Schiller shouted once more, "Take him, Pardee."

A bullet sailed past Lex, so close he thought he could feel the heat of the lead as it whistled by. Carlos limped into the open then, and Pardee scrambled to get a better shot at him, but the Mexican was already ducking back into the trees. This time Lex fired. He saw Pardee spin a half turn, the rifle cant upward. In a spasm, Pardee's finger squeezed the trigger.

Lex heard a gunshot then and jerked his eyes back to Schiller, who was standing with his back to the Ranger now. The rancher squeezed off a shot, and just beyond Schiller's hip Lex saw Carlos stagger to one side and fall to the ground.

Schiller was turning then, looking for Lex, when a

bullet slammed into him and drove the elegant rancher forward a step. His ruffled white shirt was already bloodstained where the slug had passed through him from behind. Lex was stunned for a moment, then noticed the small curl of white smoke drifting away from the muzzle of the Mexican's Colt.

Schiller's face wore a look of bafflement, and he stared down at his shirtfront, a strange calm on his features, as if a clumsy waiter had just spilled soup in his lap. He dabbed at the blood for a moment, then stared at his fingertips. A second later he toppled like a piece of timber.

Gunshots exploded all over the hillside then as Schiller's men, finally understanding what had happened, opened up on the house. Lex saw Kensington run for the building, stumble once, then crawl behind the front corner.

Lex sprinted for Carlos and knew even before he reached him that the Mexican was dead. His black eyes had an odd glaze as Lex knelt beside him. Lex closed them with his thumb and looked at the sky for a moment.

Then, from far away, he heard more gunfire and looked off across the valley, where a dozen men on horseback were charging toward the Kensington place.

He knew it was the help he'd sent for. Combined with Clayton Schiller's death, it would save Laidlaw and its people. It would save James Kensington and his farm. It would save Anna Kraus. And it would save Doc Kraus, maybe even give the old man the courage to face the rest of his life without the help of his narcotic. But it wouldn't save the one man who'd made it possible.

It was too late for Carlos Muñoz.

Dan Mason is the pseudonym of a full-time writer who lives in upstate New York with his family.

Saddle-up to these

THE REGULATOR *by Dale Colter*
Sam Slater, blood brother of the Apache and a cunning bounty-hunter, is out to collect the big price on the heads of the murderous Pauley gang. He'll give them a single choice: surrender and live, or go for your sixgun.

THE REGULATOR—Diablo At Daybreak
by Dale Colter
The Governor wants the blood of the Apache murderers who ravaged his daughter. He gives Sam Slater a choice: work for him, or face a noose. Now Slater must hunt down the deadly renegade Chacon…Slater's Apache brother.

THE JUDGE *by Hank Edwards*
Federal Judge Clay Torn is more than a judge—sometimes he has to be the jury *and* the executioner. Torn pits himself against the most violent and ruthless man in Kansas, a battle whose final verdict will judge one man right…and one man dead.

THE JUDGE—War Clouds
by Hank Edwards
Judge Clay Torn rides into Dakota where the Cheyenne are painting for war and the army is shining steel and loading lead. If war breaks out, someone is going to make a pile of money on a river of blood.

HarperPaperbacks *By Mail*

5 great westerns!

THE RANGER *by Dan Mason*
Texas Ranger Lex Cranshaw is after a killer whose weapon isn't a gun, but a deadly noose. Cranshaw has vowed to stop at nothing to exact justice for the victims, whose numbers are still growing…but the next number up could be his own.

Here are 5 Western adventure tales that are as big as all outdoors! You'll thrill to the action and Western-style justice: swift, exciting, and man-to-man!

Buy 4 or more and save!
When you buy 4 or more books, the postage and handling is FREE!

**VISA and MasterCard holders—call
1-800-331-3761
for fastest service!**

MAIL TO: **Harper Collins Publishers, P. O. Box 588, Dunmore, PA 18512-0588, Tel: (800) 331-3761**

YES, send me the Western novels I've checked:
- ☐ **The Regulator**
  0-06-100100-7....$3.50
- ☐ **The Regulator/
  Diablo At Daybreak**
  0-06-100140-6....$3.50
- ☐ **The Judge**
  0-06-100072-8 ...$3.50
- ☐ **The Judge/War Clouds**
  0-06-100131-7....$3.50
- ☐ **The Ranger**
  0-06-100110-4....$3.50

SUBTOTAL .... $_____

POSTAGE AND HANDLING* .... $_____

SALES TAX (NJ, NY, PA residents) .... $_____

Remit in US funds,
do not send cash   **TOTAL:** $_____

Name_____

Address_____

City_____

State_____ Zip_____

Allow up to 6 weeks delivery.
Prices subject to change.

*Add $1 postage/handling for up to 3 books…
FREE postage/handling if you buy 4 or more.

H0131